MISSION OF MERCY

A revolution breaks out in the independent Arab republic of Hanah. The French legation is in danger. A tiny Foreign Legion detachment is sent into the country, ordered to protect European lives and property. But that detachment is in no condition to undertake a task that calls for restraint as well as courage. It is under the command of Captain Laubert, a cunning but demented officer . . . a man who has been threatened with arrest by his junior officer.

JOHN ROBB

MISSION OF MERCY

Complete and Unabridged

LINFORD
Leicester

First published in Great Britain in 1954

First Linford Edition
published 2015

A catalogue record for this book is available
from the British Library.

ISBN 978–1–4448–2304–2

Published by
F. A. Thorpe (Publishing)
Anstey, Leicestershire

Set by Words & Graphics Ltd.
Anstey, Leicestershire
Printed and bound in Great Britain by
T. J. International Ltd., Padstow, Cornwall

This book is printed on acid-free paper

Prologue

On a February evening a cipher signal was tapped out from the French legation in the independent Arab republic of Hanah.

Hanah is on the southern borders of Algeria, roughly midway between Ain Sefra and the Territory of the Oases. It is a small country and exceptionally primitive and remote.

The signal caused a wave of anxiety when it was studied by senior civil servants in Paris. Some details of it cannot be quoted — they are still docketed as 'confidential intelligence.' But the substance ran thus:

Mobs gaining control of entire Hanah republic. Government certain to fall. Violent anti-French feeling being aroused. All French nationals have taken refuge in this legation, but legation itself may be stormed. Massacre may follow if protection does not reach us soon.

It was unexpected. And it was a first-class crisis.

The French Cabinet met for an emergency midnight sitting to consider the signal. At two o'clock in the morning there was a brief recess while officers of the General Staff were called for consultation. Shortly after three the meeting ended. At the same time the following signal was wirelessed to the General Officer Commanding, at Sidi Bel Abbes, in Algeria: —

★   ★   ★

Advised revolution in Arab republic of Hanah. French nationals in danger. Deploy a force into the territory to protect French lives and property. But do not take any action which may be interpreted as interference with internal affairs of that country. In this respect the utmost restraint must be observed. Confirmation and additional details follow by plane.

★   ★   ★

The message — for reasons which will become apparent — caused voluble fury among the staff officers at Sidi Bel Abbes.

2

The Brigadier-General summarised it when he said: 'Five years ago the place was a French protectorate and we had military bases there. And the country was at peace. But what did we do? *Ciel!* We moved out and granted it complete independence! It was absurd to grant independence to an Arab area which for a thousand years had been torn by internal strife and primitive hatreds. It was a crime . . . We soldiers said so. But we were ignored. We are always ignored. Now we are expected to clear up the mess . . . '

He threw a pencil violently onto the long conference table. A senior major retrieved it, coughed, and said softly: 'I'm told that some of the people are advanced and well able to look after their own affairs.' The Brigadier-General made an emphatic gesture.

'That is true — but it is no argument. It is always vital to decide policies in favour of well-meaning minorities. In the end they are always destroyed by the evil majority. That is what's happening now in Hanah.' A colonel said: 'I was stationed there in the old days. It's a foul place.

Mostly desert, but in the south-west there's a belt of jungle with the foliage so thick it takes a full day to march five miles. And there's only one town — that's Baikas, the capital. A stinking spot. If it weren't for the silver mines nearby I don't suppose there'd be a single Frenchman living there.'

The Brigadier-General looked at the colonel with interest.

'About how many French nationals are resident in Hanah?' he asked.

'No more than forty.'

'All men, I suppose.'

'*Non*. When I was there a few women were among the white community. Mostly wives of mining engineers.'

'No children, I trust?'

'No children, *mon generale*. The climate is too unhealthy.'

The Brigadier-General sighed. He gazed at his staff thoughtfully. When he spoke again he did so slowly being in the happy position of knowing that no one would interrupt him.

He said: 'It would be foolish, gentle-men, to think of moving a large force into the country — even if we had a large force available. We must remember that a long column of heavily-armed legionnaires would have the appearance of an invasion, and the Arabs would resent it. Thus we might provoke the very incidents we are under orders to avoid. So, for this operation, a small body of men is called for. Their numbers must be just sufficient to scare the mobs away from the legation, but not enough to cause resentment. It ought not to be a difficult mission. After all, the Legion still has considerable prestige value, and prestige will count for a lot in a place like Hanah . . . '

He coughed and waited for questions.

The Major asked: 'From which base will you send the troops?'

The Brigadier-General indicated the map in front of him.

'They will be drawn from Fort Iama. That fort is small and it may cause some temporary inconvenience when part of the garrison is detached. But it is the obvious choice since it is our nearest base to the Hanah border. From there, our men ought to be able to get into Baikas within twenty-four hours.'

'Who commands Fort Iama?'

'A fellow called Laubert — Captain Laubert. I haven't met him, but I've been looking at his file. He is an experienced officer with an excellent record, and due for promotion shortly. I'm sending a signal to him immediately, and I will be quite happy to leave the details of the operation in his hands . . . '

1

The Place of Hate

It was almost dawn when Legionnaire Zicco decided to kill himself. The sun was not yet visible, but it warned of its coming, for there was a tinge of grey in the blue-black sky.

Zicco leaned against the ramparts. He thrust back his kepi and let the breeze play upon his brow. The action was an offence against Standing Orders for Sentries at Fort Iama. But now Zicco was no longer over-awed by orders. Nothing mattered any more . . .

He told himself that soon the livid sun would be torturing all within those sandstone walls. But it would not be torturing Zicco.

Soon, within the compound, men under training schedules would be sweating like market swine. But Zicco would not sweat.

And soon Captain Laubert would be taking his morning parade. But Legionnaire Zicco would not be in the ranks.

Zicco the Hungarian was a piece of human material which had reached breaking stress. He could not go on. He did not want to go on.

He felt a wave of trembling horror pass through his slight body. Yet it was not altogether unpleasant. It was as if he was being titillated by a feeble electric current. He was afraid of that which he intended doing. But there was a simultaneous sense of relief. Like the moment when one takes the first dive into a swimming pool.

Zicco whispered to himself: 'It won't hurt very much . . . anyway, it won't hurt for long . . . '

He looked about him.

His sentry beat on the east wall extended for precisely sixty-two regulation paces. There was not yet sufficient light for him to see either extremity of it. He wondered about the three other sentries — one to each wall. Did they suspect? Of course they would not.

From the adjoining south ramparts he heard a slow, monotonous sound. *Crunch! Crunch! Crunch!*

That would be Sayle, the Englishman. He was a restless one, was Legionnaire Sayle. On sentry duty the others moved as little as possible. But Sayle was seldom still.

Below, in the centre of the square compound, he could just discern the shadowy mass of the compound buildings. Ominous, unkind buildings. He shivered again. The greater part of those buildings were taken up by the garrison mess hall, where the men slept, ate, gambled and argued. At the moment, most of them would be sleeping. Poor devils! They would not escape the misery of the day.

Zicco sniffed. There was a tang of smoke in his nostrils. That would be coming from the kitchen. Cook-Corporal Makaat must be up and preparing for the day. Lighting the vast kerosene stove and heating weak coffee. Bitter coffee with too much chicory.

Time was passing . . .

He must not wait too long.

Zicco looked diffidently at his Lebel — a long and cumbersome weapon. Not ideal for his purpose.

He pressed free the safety catch, put the heel of the butt between his boots. Then he rested his forehead against the upright muzzle. It felt hard and cool like an estranged lover's kiss.

He stretched down for the trigger.

And little that was recognisable remained of Zicco.

Under the impetus of reflex nervous action, his almost headless body performed a momentary jig on the rampart ledge. Then it fell through thirty feet of semi-darkness into the compound.

★   ★   ★

It echoed briefly, that single cordite explosion. Just long enough to mask the thud as Zicco's body smote the ground. There followed a short period of intense unnatural silence.

On the ramparts . . .

Legionnaire Brian Sayle was approaching the western extremely of his beat;

therefore he had his back to Zicco's wall. He wheeled round, his hand tightening on the rifle sling. But he did not free the Lebel from his shoulder. Not immediately. He stood very still, staring towards the east ramparts. Waiting for a call from Zicco. Waiting for some indication of what had happened.

Then quite suddenly — and for no reason except that of pure instinct — he knew. And he swore.

When he had uttered the last imprecation, Sayle thrust back his shoulders and whispered to himself: 'It had to happen . . . it could happen to any of us in this place . . .'

In the guardroom . . .

Seven legionnaires were playing a desultory game of *vingt-et-une* with a pack of forty-three limp cards. Of the remaining five members of the night guard, three were dozing on wall bunks and two were arguing about the virtue (or lack of virtue) of Marseilles women. And Sergeant Horfal, the Spaniard, was making a formal entry in the report book.

The atmosphere in the confined space

was heavy with sweaty heat, for the door was still closed against the night air. Thus the Lebel shot was heard by them as a muffled crash.

The card players became rigid. The dozing legionnaires flicked open their heavy eyes but remained still. The argument ceased.

And Sergeant Horfal let his pen remain dipped in its chipped pot of ink.

The collective immobility lasted for perhaps five seconds. Then it seemed that they all acted at once. Horfal threw down the pen and gave the order, but there was no need for it. The legionnaires were already buttoning *capotes* and pulling on equipment. Within half a minute they were streaming across the compound to their alarm stations.

The three men whose posting was on the east ramparts found Zicco. His body lay within a few yards of the steps.

They huddled round him, bewildered, horrified. Then, remembering Standing Orders, they clattered up to the ramparts.

When they looked down, Sergeant Horfal was peering over the shattered, scarlet mess. The Spaniard's lean, slightly scarred face had suddenly become sunken at the cheeks. There was a primeval savagery in his fine brown eyes.

'This,' he said, 'is murder . . . gentle murder after many games of roulette . . . '

In Captain Laubert's bunk . . .

The captain was sitting back in his canvas chair, his short, fat legs resting on his battered desk. He still wore pyjamas, although he had risen from his bed in the corner more than an hour before. A blue dressing gown was draped cloak-like over his fleshy shoulders.

An oil lamp spluttered from the low ceiling.

He was inspecting his photographs.

A pile of several dozen glossy pictures reposed on his lap. He lingered over some of them, his thick lips slack.

Others were thrown more quickly to join the scattered assortment on the floor.

Occasionally Laubert would mutter an appreciation.

'Superb . . . magnificent! Such legs . . . '

These were what Laubert described as 'the ladies of my art gallery.' All of them portrayed young women in various advanced stages of undress. The type of pictures that appear regularly in the more sophisticated magazines. Not indecent, but certainly not entertainment for prudes.

Laubert lingered exceptionally long over a portrait of a girl clad in little save black fishnet stockings. The printed inscription beneath said 'Collette.' That was all. Otherwise, the model was entirely anonymous. Which was a pity, Laubert thought. For here was female perfection. Tall, but not too tall. Slender yet with an emphatic shape. A hint of arrogance, a suggestion of mischief. The sort of woman he had never been able to resist.

He snorted when at last he threw down the picture. His flaccid round face was sweating. He licked his mouth with the tip of a curiously pink tongue.

This, he told himself, was ridiculous.

He, Laubert, was the sort of man who could not live without the company of women. Beautiful women. Poised women. They were to him what wine was to some men, food to others. They were a necessity. Yet for two years now he had been on garrison fort duty. He had been isolated from these vital, most necessary creatures. True, he had had occasional leave periods in Algiers or Oran. But they had been too short. They had served only to stimulate his appetite. And now . . . now he was reduced to this. Reduced to staring at pictures.

He stood up, the portraits cascading from his lap. He crossed to the window, which faced east. There was a barely-detectable smudge of grey in the sky. Soon another day would be here. Another vile period of heat and sweat in this remote, preposterous outpost. Surrounded only by men. Crude men, most of them. *Dieu!* How he hated men! How he longed to see the soft and gracious form of a lovely female . . .

On the east ramparts he could just discern the outline of a sentry. A slightly-built sentry. He realized that it must be the Hungarian, Zicco. For Zicco, he recalled, had been on the evening picket parade. And there was no mistaking that tiny figure, even when seen in silhouette. Zicco must have satisfied the minimum physical requirements of the Legion with nothing to spare.

Laubert laughed softly as he thought of

the Hungarian. *Tiens!* What a preposterous fellow he was! Sensitive, nervous. He should never have become a soldier. Still, Zicco could not complain that his captain was not taking an interest in him. Every day he had Zicco in his office, teaching him Russian roulette. Making a man of him . . .

Laubert was smiling quite broadly as he thought of the Russian roulette episodes with Zicco. They were most entertaining. And, oddly enough, the spectacle of the Hungarian being reduced to gibbering terror did him a lot of good. It made him, Laubert, feel a stronger and less dissatisfied man; made him forget, temporarily, his yearning for a civilised life.

It was such an interesting game, this Russian roulette. He and Zicco played it together with an old Smith and Wesson revolver. He loaded the gun with one. round — just one. He closed his eyes. Then he gave the chamber a spin. When it stopped whirling round he pressed it to his head and pulled the trigger. Since, when full, the revolver held six rounds, the theoretical chances were six to one against killing oneself.

But, in fact, the odds against sudden death were even less than that, for the chamber tended to come to rest with the weight of the cartridge at the bottom and away from the hammer.

Many times he had pointed this out to Zicco. But Zicco had not been reassured. The Hungarian always watched with pop-eyed horror while Laubert performed on himself. Then he was reduced to jellified pulp when ordered to do the same thing.

And Laubert saw that he did it. It was fascinating to see the agony on the little fellow's face as he held the gun to his head and squeezed the trigger. Most amusing to observe the relief which spread over him when the only result was a mechanical click.

'It's this life that makes me seek amusement in such things,' he told himself as he started at the ramparts. 'I must have excitement. Any sort of excitement is better than none at all. They should never have posted me to a place like this. If I'm kept here much longer I'll go mad . . .'

He broke off because Legionnaire

Zicco seemed to be doing a jig on the ramparts. And at the same moment he heard the echoing crash of a Lebel shot.

Laubert saw Zicco fall from the ledge and vanish into the deep shadows.

★   ★   ★

They buried Zicco deep in the rough red sand at ten o'clock that morning. His body was enclosed in four blankets and a Tricolour was placed over it. Lieutenant Du Pois, the second in command, read the prescribed service. Then twenty legionnaires fired a salute over the grave.

Captain Laubert had not put in an appearance. He was still in his bunk.

When they were back in the fort, Lieutenant Du Pois dismissed the burial squad. He was about to enter the compound buildings when the medical officer emerged. The M.O. was normally a cheerful, middle-aged man. Now he looked strained, old.

He said to Du Pois: 'I want to speak to you — alone.'

They turned from the buildings. They

18

walked near the fort walls, where there was little chance of being overheard. But, like conspirators, they kept their voices down.

The M.O. said: 'I've spoken to you before about Laubert. I told you something like this would happen.'

'I know you did.'

'You must do something.'

'Do what?'

'You're the second in command. You have certain rights under the French Articles of War.'

Du Pois lit a cigarette. His hands were shaking. He was young, unsure, frightened.

'I've read the clauses that you're thinking about. They are just words, words . . . '

'But there is power in those words. Legal power which entitles you to relieve an unfit officer of his command. And Laubert is unfit. I am a doctor, and am ready to give you a written certificate saying so.'

Du Pois inhaled deeply, like a man seeking relief in a drug.

'Would you say he is physically unfit for his duties?'

'*Non.* Not physically.'

'Then you must mean mentally.'

'But of course! I have explained to you many times — he is a plain case of functional psychosis bordering on paranoia. In plain terms, *mon ami*, he is the type of man who slowly goes mad under the stress of prolonged periods of isolation.'

'Then he should not have become a soldier.'

'There would have been no trace of the tendency in early life. Usually it only emerges in middle age. Now Laubert hungers intensely for the physical pleasures. He resents the fact that he cannot taste them. But he finds some satisfaction in inflicting fear on the men under his command. That is why he played Russian roulette with the wretched Zicco. It afforded him real pleasure to see a naturally-timid little fellow like Zicco suffer. And how he must have suffered! Obviously, he shot himself so as to escape yet another ghastly charade with Laubert's pistol.'

They had drawn level with the guardroom, which was under the gates. Several sentries were grouped around here, and a fatigue party was painting the guardroom door. The men had a vaguely sullen aspect. Du Pois and the M.O. ceased talking until they were out of their hearing.

Then Du Pois said: 'I'll make a report when we are relieved, of course. Laubert's conduct has been highly improper. There'll be a court of inquiry, and I think that'll be the end of him.'

The M.O. snorted.

'When we are relieved! When will that be?'

'In about two months.'

'Then you propose to let this madman remain in command for two months! It is absurd! You must know the mood of the garrison even now — it is ugly. They know what Zicco endured. And they know why Zicco killed himself. They are not fools. They hate Laubert.'

Du Pois threw down his half-smoked cigarette. His brain was whirling. He had less than two years seniority in his rank, and this was his first spell of fort duty. So far as experience went, he was a military chicken. Yet here he was being urged to invoke the Articles of War, which dealt with Lunacy or other Mental Incapacity and place a senior captain like Laubert under open arrest! He gave an involuntary shudder at the thought. Du Pois was no coward, but he could not visualise himself even attempting such a thing, much less carrying it to a successful conclusion.

He said without much conviction: 'It may all blow over. After all, Laubert has never bothered about the other legionnaires. It was only Zicco that he tortured.'

'He will find another! He *must* have someone! And he will choose one like Zicco . . . the legionnaires are hard and tough, I know. But in every garrison there is always a handful who are less hard, less tough than the rest. Laubert will find one of them. He will force him to play that abominable game. Then . . . then one day, *mon ami*, we may have real trouble in Fort Iama.'

'You mean?'

'*Oui*. I mean we could have a mutiny. And speaking as a doctor, I would have some sympathy with mutineers.'

☆　☆　☆

About thirty men were off duty. Most of them sprawled on their bunks, stripped to the waist. They were breathing quickly and shallowly under the sapping fury of the midday heat. They were watching a macabre little ceremony.

Two N.C.O.s were checking and assembling the equipment and personal possessions of the late Legionaire Zicco.

Cook-Corporal Makaat was giving a name to each item as he took it from the dead legionnaire's shelf. And Sergeant Horfal was ticking them off from a list before transferring them to a sack.

'Spare pair of boots . . . '

'Six letters, postmark Budapest . . . '

'One bougeron . . . '

'A civilian-type safety razor and five blades . . . '

So it went on.

Horfal separated the military and personal possessions into opposite sides of the sack. The property of the Republic would go back to garrison stores. The rest, in due time, would find its way to the Records

23

Department at Sidi Bel Abbes. Then it would be sent to Zicco's next of kin — if anything was known of his next of kin.

Finally, the sergeant and the corporal rolled up the thin straw mattress. They left that at the head of the now bare and grim-looking bunk. The legionnaires continued to watch — unmoving, un-blinking.

Sergeant Horfal glanced swiftly around him. He was sweating generously. His scarred, copper-brown face was slightly mottled. Horfal was very worried.

He recognized a dangerous atmosphere. He had come across atmospheres like this before. But never so obvious. Never so bad. And he had been soldiering for nearly thirty years.

Deliberately, he looked into the eyes of several of the legionnaires. They did not turn away. They looked straight back at him. There was no hostility in their expressions. Just point blank enquiry. They wanted to know where he stood, what he thought. It was natural enough. But Horfal knew that he must not give them even a hint of his true feelings. His loyalty must be to the commanding officer. That was the whole basis of his rank.

But . . .

He recognized that he must say something. To walk out now, ignoring the whole tragedy of Zicco, would be callous and stupid. And Horfal had neither of those faults. He was hard. But he was shrewd and just.

He cleared his throat. It was a nervous reaction. Then he said quietly: 'I am sorry about Zicco. He was a good comrade. I think we are all sorry about him.'

There was a shuffle of movement from a bunk at the far corner. Horfal saw Legionnaire Sayle get to his feet.

Sayle was wiping his body with a square of towel as he said: 'Is Captain Laubert sorry, too?'

Horfal had been half-expecting this. And he'd had an idea the question would come from the Englishman. There was a touch of restless arrogance about this lean, tall man which made it natural for him to take the lead in such matters. In his confidential moments, Horfal some-times admitted to himself that he was puzzled by Legionnaire Sayle. Obviously, he was a well-educated man — he spoke French almost as fluently as a native, and it was rumoured that he spoke several other tongues, too. It was equally obvious that he had an excellent brain. Sayle must have been someone quite important before he enlisted — but no one enquired too closely about such things in the Legion. Horfal contented himself with the knowledge that, on the whole, he liked the man.

But he did not like him at this moment for the sharply-pointed question. He controlled a surge of annoyance. This was no time to take advantage of rank. He must be informal.

'I said we are all sorry, legionnaire.'

'I know, *mon sergeant*. But Zicco was murdered. Murdered because of a game of roulette.'

Horfal recalled that he had said something very similar only a few hours ago as he stood over the mutilated body. The realization gave him a shock.

'I cannot talk about such wild ideas, legionnaire. What happened to Zicco has happened to others before him. Perhaps the isolation and the strain drove him temporarily mad.'

'Zicco was not mad. He was scared and tortured to a point where he did not dare to go on living. But what about our commanding officer? Do you think he is sane, *mon sergeant*?'

'Legionnaire! I may have to put you under arrest if you speak that way!'

Horfal regretted having to do the very thing he had decided to avoid. But he could conceive of no other way out of this situation. Sayle's questions were directed at him like the suave interrogation of a skilled lawyer. And he felt the eyes of the others gazing upon him. Coldly curious eyes. Those men could be dangerous. Horfal licked his lips. For the first time, he loathed the *galons* of his rank. He wished he could speak freely. To tell the men that he thought as they thought . . .

Sayle seemed to be unmoved by the reprimand. He threw the towel on his bunk. Then he gestured towards a small, plump legionnaire who was standing incon- spicuously beside him. Horfal recognized

Legionnaire Katz — the Austrian Jew. Katz was a mild, thoughtful type of man. The sort of man who did everything quietly, without fuss. There had been a complete absence of fuss about the way Katz had won the *Medaille Militaire* a year before for gallantry in Indo-China. If his heroism on that occasion had not been seen by a senior officer, there would have been no decoration. For Katz certainly would not have spoken of what he had done, and he would have sincerely urged us comrades not to do so.

Sayle said: 'Katz thinks he may be the next to be invited to a game of Russian roulette.'

Horfal gave a half-controlled gasp. 'What are you talking about? What gives you this foolish idea?'

'Katz gave it to me. I had to drag it out of him — but I daresay he'll tell you for himself.'

Under his tan there was a pink hue in Katz's round face. He did not speak.

Horfal stared hard at him.

'Well, Katz — what is this?'

Kate swallowed. He glanced at Sayle.

His expressive features showed regret that Sayle had spoken with appreciation for the motives which had made him do so. Then he said: 'It is true, *mon sergeant*. I — I think. I may be ordered to play with the revolver.'

'Why?'

'Two weeks ago the captain asked me if I'd heard of the game. I said I had.'

'Is that all?'

'Yes. And I think it is enough, *mon sergeant*.'

Horfal found that he was breathing noisily. It *was* enough, he admitted to himself. Katz, with his mild appearance, would be the very sort of man that Lauber would select . . . But it was obvious that Laubert did not know much about Katz. He was a different specimen in many ways to the wretched Zicco

Horfal decided that it would be useless to go on with the pretence that Laubert's revolver game did not exist.

He asked: 'And if you are right — if you are ordered to play Russian roulette — what will you do, legionnaire?'

Katz said softly: 'I will refuse. I will say

29

that it is an improper order.'

A stir of movement went round the mess room. All the men were now standing. Some of them gave vague grunts of approval.

Horfal felt a stab of pain in his forehead. It came from the place where he had been wounded during the Spanish Civil War. It only bothered him when he was intensely worried. He thought: 'We are sitting on a volcano — all of us. If nothing is done, it will erupt. I will have to speak to Du Pois. There must be a way out . . . I'm sure the Articles of War provide somewhere for madness in a commanding officer . . . '

But Horfal said: 'I want you to forget about Captain Laubert. I will see that no one is ordered to take part in such foolishness. I promise it . . . and I speak to you as a man to other men . . . '

An orderly came through the doorway. He came to attention opposite Horfal.

'Order from Captain Laubert,' he said. 'He directs Legionnaire Katz to report immediately to his bunk.'

2

Edge of Decision

A phrase from his native Spanish tongue emerged from nowhere. It clashed like an ill-tuned cymbal in Horfal's aching head.

Guerra al cuchillo!

War to the knife!

Was that what Laubert was creating? Was he forcing a situation in which even the loyalty and authority of his officers and N.C.O.s would be shattered? Did he in his madness realise that he was driving the garrison to mutiny? Soldiers, Horfal knew well enough, would tolerate massive amounts of purely physical hardship and injustice without showing even a trace of insubordination. But unnatural and selective mental torture like this was something they could never understand. They would lash against it as men strike out wildly at unseen enemies in the dark.

Horfal looked at Katz. The Austrian

Jew was pulling on his tunic. There was nothing hurried, yet no hesitancy about the action. He was calm. Probably the calmest one there. His fingers were steady as he fastened the buttons. It was the same when he buckled his bayonet belt. And when he laced his boots. He produced a piece of cloth to give his boots a polish. That done, he reached for his *kepi*, blew dust off it, settled it firmly on his head.

Then he squared his shoulders.

Probably it was that gesture which forced Horfal to the critical decision. There was something brave yet helpless about the way Katz had moved those shoulders. It symbolised a man who knew he would suffer, but who would not be conquered.

Horfal's voice had regained its parade ground crispness as he said: 'You will stay here, Legionnaire Katz.'

Katz looked surprised, a little confused.

Horfal repeated: 'You will stay here. You will not report to Captain Laubert.'

'But . . . but it is an order. I must obey . . . '

'You said you would refuse to obey him.'

'Yes, *mon sergeant*, if he expected me to play with the revolver. I'd be in my military rights in doing so, because it would be an improper order. But this . . . this is just an instruction for me to report to him. I will have to do as he says.'

Horfal paused. Then he said: 'Answer me carefully — in your heart do you know why he wants to see you?'

'Yes . . . I think I know.'

'He expects you to take the place of Zicco. You know what that means. He'll put just one round in the revolver, spin the chamber and fire at his own head. Then he'll order you to do the same. You will refuse. He'll have you put under arrest. It will be a long, long time before you can expect to face the justice of a court-martial. Much could happen to you while you waited.'

'I know that.'

'But you will not take a chance? You will not satisfy a perverted craze by pulling the trigger?'

'No, *mon sergeant*, I will not.'

'There is not much risk. The weight of the cartridge . . . '

'I know, *mon sergeant*. But it is not just a matter of the risk. I think that — that dignity comes into it. Even a soldier is entitled to that. My people believe that without dignity a man is nothing.'

Horfal nodded slowly.

'Very well, Katz. My order stands. You will not report to the captain.'

Katz made a desperate gesture.

'But I'll have to! He is . . . and you . . . '

'You mean that he is the commanding officer and I am only the senior N.C.O. So his orders are superior to mine. In the ordinary way that is so. But in military usage you must obey the last order you receive. Your last order is from me. It is to take off your tunic and *stay here*! You will have nothing to fear. The responsibility is mine. I will answer to our commanding officer!'

Then, suddenly, Sergeant Horfal had turned about and was gone.

⋆　⋆　⋆

Lieutenant Du Pois had a tiny bunk next to the fort kitchen. The room stank perpetually of coffee and salted meat.

In addition to the bed, the furnishings consisted only of one chair and a tarnished shaving mirror. There was scarcely space for more. The place was exceptionally crowded now, for Du Pois was entertaining the Medical Officer.

The M.O. — in deference to his years — was on the chair. Du Pois sat on a corner of the bed. Both were concentrating on the Manual of the Articles of War which, for mutual convenience, lay open on the stone floor.

As he crouched over it, Du Pois realised that the clauses that they were studying were astoundingly clear.

They began by laying it down that *'Circumstances may arise when it may become necessary to relieve a commanding officer of his duties without reference to higher authority . . . '*

Then later: *'If a commanding officer is suddenly beset by a mental or nervous affliction of such a character as to prevent him efficiently carrying out his duties, the* officer next in seniority will take over the functions of command. He may put the afflicted officer under such restraint as may be necessary for his own safety and military efficiency . . . '

And later still: 'Such action will only be taken by a junior officer when no other course is reasonably possible, and after heeding medical advice, where such advice is available . . . '

There followed a clause stating that in all such cases a High Command Enquiry into the circumstances would be held, presided over by an officer not under the rank of Brigadier General.

Here, in official print, Du Pois was confronted by the fact that he had the power to take over from Laubert. He had the power because he had the justification. And he was horrified by the prospect.

But here was the Medical Officer arguing with him. Always trying to persuade him.

'Is not Laubert's conduct an outrage?' the M.O. vas asking. 'Madness apart, has he not lost all right to the respect of his garrison?'

Du Pois did not answer. The M.O. would not be fobbed off with silence.

'I was asking you if Laubert has not . . . ?'

'*Oui*. I think his conduct is an outrage.'

'And he is crazed. Perhaps it is only temporary, but that does not matter. As a doctor I know that a man only does the things he has done under the stress of lunacy — but I have tried to explain my diagnosis to you . . . he is a case of repression. He suffers the effects of isolation.'

Du Pois asked: 'Do you mean that if he had some new interest . . . some sort of action to occupy his mind . . . he would recover?'

'Probably. I think he would become normal almost immediately. But there is no prospect of that happening here, *mon ami*. In Fort Iama there is only heat and loneliness and routine. It has driven other men mad before Laubert.'

Du Pois extended a foot and closed the Manual. He hated the thing. It told him of that which he ought to do, but hardly dared to do.

If only he had a few more years of

experience on his shoulders! If only he were not utterly afraid of Laubert! If only he had never been sent to this damned fort at all!

He croaked: 'I wish I could send a radio signal to Bel Abbes explaining . . . '

The M.O. said: 'You can do that when you have taken over command. Not before.'

That was the hellish truth, Du Pois told himself. Under Standing Orders no radio signal could be transmitted without the authority of the Commanding Officer. Certainly the wireless operator would refuse to transmit any signal that was not signed by Laubert himself. In any case, such action would be an admission of cowardice. The officers at Bel Abbes could do nothing except tell him to act under the provisions of the Articles. They were more than a thousand miles away. *Non*, the time to send a signal was after he had screwed up the courage to face Laubert and put him under restraint.

But would he ever have the courage?

Du Pois decided to take the easy and obvious way out.

'I'll wait a few days,' he said. 'Laubert may recover.'

The M.O. threw up his hands.

'It may be fatal to wait! I have told you that . . . ' He broke off. The sound of quick footsteps rang from the outer corridor. There was an indefinable sug- gestion of urgency about them. They stopped outside the closed door. Then there was a sharp rap on the panel.

Du Pois drew in a breath to invite the person in. There was no need. Before he could speak, the door was thrust open.

Sergeant Horfal strode in.

A tense, almost ferocious Sergeant Horfal.

He did not advance into the room, for there was hardly space for him to do so. But he eased slightly beyond the thresh- old. There he saluted briefly.

And, after glancing at the Medical Officer, he fixed his eyes on Du Pois and said: 'Permission to make a report, *mon officier?*'

Du Pols nodded.

'Certainly, sergeant. What is it?'

'Captain Laubert has ordered Legion- naire Katz to his bunk.'

Du Pois looked puzzled. 'Well . . . ? What of it?'

Horfal's voice grated. He said: 'I believe it is to play Russian roulette . . . I am certain of it.'

Du Pois wore a cheap but reliable American wristwatch. Its ticking suddenly became clearly audible.

A junior corporal was taking a squad in arms drill at the far end of the compound. His words of command suddenly became shrilly clear.

In the adjoining kitchen an orderly was having trouble with the kerosene stove. His mumbled curses penetrated the wall.

It was the M.O. who spoke first.

'What makes you certain about the roulette, sergeant?'

Horfal told him.

'This man Katz . . . is he with Laubert now?'

'*Non, mon officier.* I countermanded the order.'

Du Pois blinked, astonished.

'You did that! You had no authority.'

'I know that. But I had no choice. If Katz had gone in there . . . and if there had been an accident with the gun when he pulled the trigger . . . '

Horfal left the sentence unfinished. The M.O. completed it for him.

'You mean there might have been trouble with the garrison?'

'I mean there would have been a mutiny.'

'So!' The M.O. stared hard at Du Pois. Then he added: 'Does that not support what I've already told you?'

Du Pois nodded wearily.

The M.O. went on: 'He does not even wait for one victim to cool in his grave before he seeks another. *Tiens!* His condition is even worse than I thought! You must take over from him now. You must!'

Horfal looked from one to another. Then he chanced to catch sight of the Manual on the floor. He appreciated its significance. He said to the wilting lieutenant:

'With respect, it is the only way, *mon officier*. The legionnaires — they hate Captain Laubert.'

Du Pois muttered: 'Legionnaires often hate their officers.'

'Certainly. But there are different sorts of hate. Some of it is a passing thing, like a cloud on the sun. But some hate never passes. It is never forgotten. It is in the heart and the mind, and it calls for vengeance. That is the hate the men feel.'

There was a touch of fire in the way Horfal had spoken. The fire of his native Spain.

It made an impression on Du Pois.

Gradually, the lieutenant ceased to have the aspect of a huddled wreck. He got to his feet. He adjusted his tunic, put on his kepi. The others watched intently.

He said: 'I will see Captain Laubert. I will relieve him of his command.'

Both the Medical Officer and Horfal gave a faint, involuntary sigh.

The M.O. said: 'I'll go with you.'

'So will I,' said Horfal.

Du Pois gave a brief, humorless smile. Then, as an afterthought, he took down his pistol holster from a nail over the bunk. He strapped it to his belt before leading the way out of the room.

★   ★   ★

42

Laubert tossed a small can of oil onto his desk. He had lubricated the revolver. Now the heavy chamber was spinning beautifully. A good flick, and it would spin ten, perhaps fifteen times. And no sound from it except a slight purr.

He inserted one cartridge into the gun.

Again he flicked the chamber, this time putting the muzzle to his head. Patiently, he waited for the revolutions to cease. At last they did so.

He told himself that this was the moment of truth. The time of utter, fascinating excitement. He was challenging the wheel of fate, and death was the stake. No boredom now. No yearning for women, for wine, for the desires of the flesh. No wild craving for release from sapping routine.

Laubert pressed the trigger.

He felt the revolver vibrate slightly as the chamber turned and the hammer jumped back.

Click!

That was all!

He had won again! Magnificent!

He broke the gun and inspected it. As

usual, the cartridge was near the bottom of its travel and well away from the breech. But the chance of death had been there. A remote chance, but none the less real because of that. Taking into account the effect of the bullet's weight, it was probably about twenty to one against.

Still holding the weapon, Laubert extended his right hand. It was rock steady. Bon! His nerve was superb.

Idly, he wondered why he had gained even more pleasure from watching Zicco have to go through this performance than he did in inflicting it on himself. He could think of no reason for it. It was a delicious sensation to see the miserable little fellow spin the chamber, then put the gun to his head. And the more frightened Zicco had been, the more he, Laubert, had enjoyed watching him.

Now this other legionnaire was coming. What was his name? Ah, *oui!* Katz.

Katz, he gathered, was a man with a good combat record. But he was obviously a quiet, docile fellow. He would offer even better entertainment than Zicco.

Where was Katz?

It must be twenty minutes since he had sent the order for him to report! This was intolerable . . .

Ah, here he was. Boots were clanking towards the room.

But what was this?

He heard several pairs of boots. And he had ordered that Katz was to report alone.

Laubert did not have time for further conjecture. There was not even a knock on the door. It was opened violently. Du Pois entered. That surprised Laubert. But he was slightly bewildered when he saw the Medical Officer and Sergeant Horfal. Laubert stared at them across his desk. Du Pois showed all the symptoms of a man who had screwed up the nerve to ace an unpleasant event. His lower lip trembled. But his eyes were steady. He stood a little in front of the others.

He said quickly: '*Capitaine*, Sergeant Horfal tells me that you have ordered a Legionnaire Katz to report to you. The order has been cancelled.'

As he listened, with fast developing aston-ishment, Laubert suddenly realised that the three men were not looking directly at him. He followed the line of their gaze. They were watching the revolver. It was still in his hand. He decided to keep it there.

'Who cancelled the order, lieutenant?'

'Sergeant Horfal — acting under my authority.'

'Really! And why?'

'Because I have reason to believe that you intend to make improper use of your rank.'

Du Pois was faintly surprised by his own fluency. He felt a growing confidence. With the M.O. and the sergeant behind him, Laubert did not seem so terrible as he had expected.

Laubert eased his weighty figure back in his chair. The canvas creaked. He said very softly: 'Go on, lieutenant. I am waiting.'

'It is known that you often forced Legionnaire Zicco to aim a loaded pistol at himself. I think you were intending to make Katz do the same. Such conduct is intolerable, so . . . '

'So you know about the roulette?'

Laubert seemed genuinely surprised.

'But of course, *capitaine*. Everyone knows. The garrison is in a dangerous mood. And you are certainly a very sick man. For that reason I am relieving you of your command under the provisions of clauses thirty to thirty-seven of the Articles of War. You will be placed under the care of the Medical Officer in the sick bay until arrangements can be made for your transfer to base. I will now radio a full report of the circumstances to Bel Abbes. You will receive a duplicate of that report as soon as it has been transmitted.'

Du Pois had spoken quite firmly, but in the manner of a man repeating well-rehearsed lines.

Laubert smiled. The smile became more expansive as he began to twirl the revolver round his forefinger.

Then he broke into a laugh.

It was a deep laugh, which came from the depth of his broad belly. His whole stocky figure shook. He used his cuff to wipe moisture from his eyes.

Du Pois's lower lip started to quiver anew. He glanced desperately at the M.O.

and Horfal, then back to Laubert.

For this was not the obvious and hysterical laugh of a madman. It was the laughter of a man who was vastly amused. Du Pois felt his recent confidence ebbing away. He was frightened again. He had expected Laubert to react with a raging fury. He could have handled that. But to be laughed at . . .

Gradually — very gradually — the sound subsided.

But Laubert had not lost his smile as he said: 'You are a very silly boy! If you were my son I think I would spank you! But as you are supposed to be a soldier under my command, I must consider other measures. I do not blame you entirely, for you are very young and you have had pressure put on you . . . I think I know who to blame for that . . . '

He looked at the Medical Officer and at Sergeant Horfal. And his smile was gone.

The M.O. stepped forward so that he was half a pace in front of Du Pois. He spoke very quietly, very firmly. And he said: 'Du Pois is doing his duty, and you will not turn him from his course by pouring ridicule upon him. Mentally, you are ill. You must face the fact. It would be best if you relinquished your command with good grace so that the garrison can return to normal as soon as possible. But whatever you say will not change the fact that, following medical advice, Lieutenant Du Pois has taken over from you.'

Laubert ceased twirling the revolver. For a moment it hung limp, suspended from his finger through the trigger guard. And the skin of Laubert's fleshy face tightened. He showed his teeth in an almost animal expression of fury.

Then, with a flick of his wrist, he brought the revolver butt into his hand. He levelled the barrel at Du Pois.

He said: 'I have only two commissioned officers in this garrison, and it seems I am faced with an insurrection from both of them. And from my senior N.C.O. I am putting all three of you under close arrest. And I will radio a report to Bel Abbes. You will receive duplicate copies of my version as soon as it has been sent . . . '

Du Pois glanced down at his holster.

'And if you attempt to reach for your pistol, lieutenant, I will shoot you. I will shoot any of you who tries to interfere with me.'

The Medical Officer pushed back his *kepi*. He said: 'As a matter of interest, what will your version be? How will you explain your interludes of roulette?'

'Roulette? I do not know what you're talking about! Has anyone in this garrison seen me indulge in the practice?'

There was a heavy silence as they realised that no one had. The only witness had died that morning.

And another factor stood heavily in Laubert's favour.

If he called the guard and ordered the arrests, that order would almost certainly be obeyed — despite any protests. So far as the legionnaires were concerned Laubert was still the commanding officer. They would have no time to consider the implications.

True, they might rebel against Laubert later, when they realised what had happened. But that would create the very situation they wished to avoid — a fort in shambles, with possible bloodshed.

Everything had depended upon Laubert being relieved of his command in an orthodox fashion by two brother officers, and the change being formally announced to the garrison after it had happened. Then there would have been no trouble.

But now . . .

Now Laubert had seized the initiative. He was a man who craved action in any and every form. Lack of it had unhinged his mind. The sudden need for it had made him capable again. And fearless.

Du Pois cleared his throat.

'You will not command the garrison for long,' he said. 'The men loathe you. I warn you — they will mutiny.'

Laubert shrugged, keeping the revolver steady.

'I will know how to handle the men. Meantime, I am calling for the guard . . . '

He stretched his free hand to a bell-push on the corner of his desk. This, operating from a battery, rang an alarm bell in the guard room. It was then, for the first time during the interview that Sergeant Horfal spoke. Up to now, the

Spaniard had remained very still in the background. Now he stepped forward. And his words came in a soft, sibilant whisper. 'Call the guard, if you wish, *mon capitaine*. It will save us the trouble. I am going to take that pistol from you.'

'Stand back, you fool! That's an order!'

'I don't recognise your orders, *capitaine*.' Horfal stopped when less than a yard separated them. Laubert aimed the gun at the centre of the sergeant's chest.

'I don't want to kill you. I want to see you face court-martial. But I will pull this trigger if you take another step.'

Horfal's thin lips parted into a suggestion of a smile.

'Is the revolver loaded, *capitaine*?'

'Certainly.'

'Is it fully loaded, *capitaine*?'

Laubert hesitated for a fraction. Then: 'It is fully loaded, sergeant.'

'I think not, *capitaine*. That is not a French officer's automatic pistol. It is an English revolver. I think is the revolver that you use for your Russian roulette. And if that is so, it will not have more than one round it.'

'Nonsense! Will you force me to shoot you?'

'I will take my chance, *capitaine*. If there is only one round in it, the odds are that it is well away from the breech. So when you press the trigger nothing will happen. I am going to disarm you — and I will be taking the same risk that Zicco took. You like your games of Russian roulette, *capitaine*! Now play with me . . .'

Laubert glanced at the chamber. But he did not need to look. He knew that the single cartridge was at the bottom.

With his thumb he pulled the chamber round, so as to bring the bullet into the firing position. But Horfal did not allow him the necessary two or three seconds. Laubert was still fumbling when Horfal's hand closed over his wrist. The sergeant gave a slight inward twist. Laubert almost rolled out of his chair. And the gun was on the desk.

Horfal picked it up, inspected it.

'As I thought,' he said, 'only one round.'

Du Pois freed his holster cover, pulled out his own gun. He levelled it at Laubert. He said: 'There be no further argument. I see it would be unsafe to allow you any freedom. You will be confined in this room, under guard.'

But Laubert did not seem to be listening. He was gazing towards the doorway. The others looked there, too. An orderly was standing half in the room, his jaw slack, eyes startled.

Horfal gave a half-suppressed curse. It was bad that one of the legionnaires should have witnessed this scene — or part of it. Exaggerated versions of what had occurred would certainly spread through the fort.

He almost shouted at the man: 'What is it?'

The orderly thrust forward a cipher slip.

'An absolute priority signal from Bel Abbes,' he said. 'It's from the High Command.'

3

Test of Experience

Horfal immediately passed the cipher slip to Du Pois and dismissed the orderly. Du Pois said to Laubert: 'The code book, please. I need to decode this signal.'

'I will decode the signal. It is sent to me.'

'It is sent to the commanding officer. I am the commanding officer.'

Possibly because of curiosity as to what the signal contained, Laubert did not argue further. He produced a bunch of keys from his tunic pocket, unlocked a desk drawer, and extracted a slim volume. Du Pois took it from him.

Judging it safe to do so, he put his pistol back in its holster, then crossed to the window-shelf. There, having established the code for the day, he set to work breaking down the signal.

The others watched in silence as Du

Pois scribbled on a scrap of paper with a pencil.

They saw his face assume a greyish tinge as one decoded word followed another.

They saw that his lower lip was pulsating even more violently than it had done earlier.

And when Du Pois had at last finished, they heard him give a short, desperate sob.

Laubert was on his feet. He stretched out an eager hand for the decoded version. 'Give me that,' he said.

But for the moment Du Pois ignored him. He handed the paper to the doctor. And Horfal, ignoring military convention, looked over the M.O.'s shoulder. When they had read it, Horfal said something incomprehensibly lurid in Spanish.

By now, Laubert was desperate with curiosity.

'What is it? *Tiens*! Let me see the thing!'

Du Pois nodded, and the message was handed to him. Laubert settled himself in his canvas chair before studying the message. Then he applied himself to it closely clearly digesting the implications of each sentence before passing on to the next. There was a new and unexpected air of authority about him.

Eventually, he sat back and surveyed the three opposite him.

'This is a critical situation,' he said.

There was no answer. He continued: 'In essence this signal directs us to protect the lives of French subjects who are taking refuge in our legation in the Republic of Hanah. But there is more in it than that, isn't there?'

He was looking hard at Du Pois. The lieutenant said lamely: 'There certainly is . . . we have to enter the territory of an independent Arab state.'

Laubert nodded. He was now in complete charge of the proceedings. 'Quite so. And we are specifically ordered to use the utmost tact and discretion. Any clash with the population must be avoided if humanly possible.'

'That will be difficult . . . the message says a mob is already threatening the legation.'

'It will be very difficult, lieutenant. Particularly since it will be impossible to detach more than fifty men for the purpose. The success or failure of the operation depends on two factors. Do you know what they are?'

'Well, I . . . er . . . '

'Factor one — the prestige effect of Legion troops. A mere handful of men can have little actual fighting power in themselves. They must rely on the fact that they represent the entire military power of France. Now, can you tell me what the second factor is?'

Du Pois was now completely lost. He had the appearance of a schoolboy who cannot answer a teacher's questions. He stared miserably into space.

Laubert leaned forward. He said, slowly, meticulously: 'Factor two is the experience and capacity of the commanding officer. He must be an officer capable of making the correct decisions instantly and under the most difficult circumstances. He must in himself carry an air of authority, which will impress these semi-savages who appear to be seizing

control in Hanah. Now tell me, lieutenant
. . . do you consider that you have those
qualifications?'

Du Pois continued to stare dumbly.

'*Answer me!*'

It was a shout.

'*Non . . .* I do not think I have the
experience.'

'Yet you presumed a few minutes ago
to relieve me of the command of this
garrison!'

'That was different. I could not expect
such an order as this arriving.'

'I agree. It was very different. But now
— assuming that you command the fort
— you must proceed immediately with a
column into Hanah territory, reaching the
capital, Baikas, with all speed. You must
leave your second-in-command in charge
of the fort. In order of rank, that means
putting this place under the direct orders
of the Medical Officer, since I will be
under arrest. It is an interesting situation,
lieutenant. I wonder what the reaction of
the High Command will be when they
learn of it.'

Laubert had won. He could not do

otherwise. The fates were on his side, and all of them in that room knew it.

Mad or sane, there could be no doubting Laubert's innate ability as a soldier. He was also certainly possessed of a wide knowledge of men and affairs. He and only he in that fort was qualified to lead the relief column. The Command had been right to entrust the mission to him. But they would never have dreamed of entrusting it to the immature lieutenant.

Laubert allowed time for these points to sink home.

Then: 'You had better forget your dreams of greatness, lieutenant. I will continue in command. Do you understand?'

'*Oui*. I understand.'

'*Bon*. For the time being we had all better forget this comedy over the Articles of War. I will reopen the matter in due time. For the present, I will, of course, take fifty men into Hanah. You, lieutenant, will stay here . . . so in a way you will have your wish. You will command this fort.'

Du Pois flushed under the incisive insult. But Laubert had turned his attention on Horfal.

'Sergeant,' he said, 'you will accompany me as my second in command. I will leave the selection of the fifty men entirely to you. Choose the most intelligent. The task will call for brain power from all ranks.'

Horfal seemed to be looking through Laubert rather than at him as he said: 'It is my duty to warn you, *mon capitaine*, that you may find the mission more dangerous than you expect.'

'So! Why?'

'The men hate you, *capitaine*. It may not be easy to control them.'

'I am aware of that. I will rely on you, sergeant, to maintain discipline. Oh! I nearly forgot . . . there is one man who must be in the column. That is Legionnaire Katz.'

★   ★   ★

The air was heavy that afternoon when Laubert inspected his column in the compound.

Heavy because there was not a breath

61

of a breeze to ease the heat of the sullen sun. Heavy because of the fury in the minds of the fifty men.

To the eye, they were a small, perfectly-disciplined body of soldiers. Motionless in open order, Lebel rifles at the slope.

Like gigantic toy troops. Each an almost exact duplicate of the other. Each bearing a scientifically-distributed burden of equipment weighing exactly thirty-five kilos. Round each waist one hundred and twenty rounds of .300 ammunition and two and a half litres of brackish water. On each back a blanket, a tent sheet, a first-aid pack, an entrenching tool, plus rations of pemmican biscuits and dried goat meat.

So perfect to the eye. But the eye does not see all.

Despite the urgency, Laubert did not hurry his inspection. He looked carefully at each man, occasionally pausing to adjust a shoulder strap or check a water bottle. He paused longest in front of the rigid Legionnaire Katz. But he could find nothing wrong there.

Laubert paused, too, in front of

Legionnaire Sayle. Not because he expected to find any fault. Merely out of curiosity. There was a peculiar intensity about the Englishman's face. Something apart from any ordinary loathing. For a moment their eyes met. And Laubert moved on. He knew he had pinpointed the main source of danger.

* * *

Du Pois watched the column march out. He stood just within the gates, at the salute. On the ramparts, the sentries were presenting arms.

When the last file had passed through, he called '*Repos!*' The sentries ordered arms.

He watched the column for fully thirty minutes, shielding his eyes against the heat haze, which shimmered over the red sand. Then, when it was only a smudge on the south-eastern horizon, he gave orders for the great double gates to be closed.

And he walked across the compound.

His steps rang hollowly on the baked

earth. That was symbolic, he told himself. For he had been presented with a hollow victory. It was just as Laubert had said. He, Du Pois, now commanded Fort Iama. But really it was only half a fort. For half of its garrison had gone. It was a shell of a place.

All he had to do was to carry on with routine and wait.

There was nothing to worry about. Not until Laubert returned.

But he admitted to himself that he was strangely afraid. This was a new form of fear. It nibbled at his vitals. Yet it would not reveal itself.

He had almost reached the compound buildings when he halted and swung round on his heels.

Faint but familiar sounds reached his ears. There could be no mistaking them, even though they came from far off. Even though they came from the direction in which Laubert's column was marching.

They were rifle shots.

4

Divide and Slay

Legionnaire Taeti decided to shoot Laubert in the back. He reached the decision half an hour after marching out of the fort. He acted upon it immediately. Taeti was that sort of man.

He was a peculiar specimen, was Taeti. Strictly speaking, he was a Hawaiian, for he was born on the beautiful isle of Maui in the group. But he reflected a weird medley of races. There was native Polynesian blood within him. But there was Japanese blood, too. And Indian. His father had been a United States marine.

The result — as often happens in such cases — was a human misfit.

Legionnaire Taeti was the sort of man who almost perpetually dwelt upon some real or imagined injustice. He was quick to see what was wrong. He could never see what was right. He brooded . . .

That was the danger in the man. He seldom spoke out about his grievances. He merely thought. He let the acid etch in his imaginative mind. His yellow-brown face was usually sullen. But he had always performed his duties competently; And Taeti had the advantage of being a massively-built man, with a chest that seemed as wide as an arm stretch.

Taeti had a secret ambition.

Since boyhood he had nursed it within the dark recesses of his turbulent mind.

He wanted to see himself leading a revolt against tyranny.

In fact, so far as Taeti was concerned, it need not be a genuine tyranny at all. Any unpopular authority would suffice. He just wanted to be a leader. The glorious liberator who would strike off the first shackle.

But always he had been thwarted by the knowledge that no one would follow him.

Always, until now.

Now Laubert was the answer to his secret yearning.

Taeti believed quite firmly that the

legionnaires would stand with him if he struck against the captain. He had not been entirely sure of this until a few hours ago.

But recent stories and rumours that had swept the garrison left him in no doubt.

It did not matter that he personally had suffered not at all at the hands of Laubert. It did not matter that he did not know or care a jot about either the late Zicco or the quiet little Austrian, Katz. Such considerations were of trifling importance.

This was Taeti's opportunity to open the floodgates of his hate — hate against nearly everyone and everything.

He would shoot Laubert! He would strike a blow for freedom!

It was a case of a twisted mind making use of a good cause.

They were marching at ease. Legionnaire Taeti was near the front of the column and on the right of his file — therefore there was no one to restrict his movements on that side. And the fat, stocky figure of Laubert was a mere fifteen paces ahead.

He unslung his Lebel from his shoulder. He did so casually. If any of the others noticed the movement, it appeared only as if he was easing a strain.

For a few steps he held the rifle at the short trail.

He watched Laubert. Watched and stoked up his fury. The probable consequences of his plan did not occur to him.

And he could have succeeded if he had been using a less unwieldy weapon than a Lebel.

As it was, Taeti thumbed free the safety catch. So far, so good. No one could have seen him do that. But the rifle was not yet ready for firing. The pin had to be cocked, and a round thrust from the magazine into the breech. This involved jerking the bolt back and then forward. Taeti attempted to achieve this operation while making a sideways jump clear of the column.

But no man — not even a powerful man like Taeti — can jump far when burdened with a full pack.

He landed less than a foot from the line

of men. And as he landed, being off balance, he sprawled on his knees. It was from that position that he had to complete the loading and take hurried aim.

There was an interval of rather more than a full second before he fired. The bullet travelled slightly high and very wide.

The reverberating crash of the explosion brought the column to a shambling, uncertain halt. Only those in the immediate vicinity knew precisely what had happened. The others fumbled uncertainly with their Lebels. Bewildered. Waiting for a clarifying word of command.

No command came. Not immediately. But Horfal acted.

Sergeant Horfal had been marching towards the rear and on the right-hand side of the column. The moment he saw Taeti jump, he started running. His long legs moved with surprising speed. He reached Taeti as the Hawaiian was feverishly trying to reload.

Horfal drew back his boot. He swung on his other heel as he kicked. His toe-cap crashed against Taeti's lower jaw.

Taeti moaned as he slumped forward on his belly. The moan changed to a scream when his nerves reacted fully to the agonising pain of a dislocated jaw.

The column swayed. The men showed signs of breaking ranks. Horfal dealt with that. He raised his voice to a penetrating screech.

'*Gare a nous . . .* '

The column did not obey to the extent of coming fully to attention. But they became comparatively still.

Laubert arrived.

If he was shaken, he showed no sign of it. There was an air of detached curiosity about his demeanour. He looked carefully down at the writhing Taeti. Then at Horfal.

'Give me a report, sergeant!'

Horfal wiped his sweating face. There was the barest suggestion of hesitation. Then: 'Legionnaire Taeti broke ranks, *mon officier*. He fired at you.'

Laubert sucked his fatted lips.

'You saw him do this?'

'*Oui.*'

'I commend you on your prompt action.'

Horfal looked uneasy. He did not

appear to appreciate the commendation.

Laubert looked again at Taeti. The Hawaiian was now on his knees again. With one hand he was probing his distorted and contused face. His initial scream had diminished into a low, continuous sob.

Laubert rapped at him: 'Stand up!'

Taeti either did not hear the command or chose to ignore it.

'Help him up, sergeant.'

Horfal stooped, put two arms under Taeti's shoulders. He hoisted him to an approximately erect position. Taeti was able to remain thus without support. But he was swaying. A lesser man would have been unconscious.

Laubert said to him: 'Have you anything to say?'

No answer.

'You are accused of attempting to murder an officer while on operational duty. I am bound by military law to consider anything you may say in your defence. If you wish to speak, do so now. You will not have another opportunity.'

Taeti raised his unlovely face and looked at Laubert. But he made no sound, save to continue his faint sobbing.

Laubert raised his voice. It was clearly heard by every legionnaire. 'Under these circumstances I have absolute power of punishment. That is laid down in the Articles you are familiar with the Articles, Sergeant Horfal You can confirm that.'

Horfal ignored the thrust.

Laubert continued: 'Normally, I might be disposed to waive my rights and have you held for a general court-martial, which would either sentence you to death or to life imprisonment. But the circumstances are not normal. It has already been explained to you, with all the others that we are on a mission of the utmost importance and urgency. The lives of many French citizens are in danger. We must reach them with all speed. I cannot tolerate even the smallest infraction of discipline. As for an attempt at murder . . . I have no choice . . . '

He paused, drew his stocky figure very straight, then added with a touch of formality: 'Under the power granted and deputed to me by the Republic of France I sentence you to death, the sentence to be carried out now.'

As the final words pierced the arid air, two separate but closely-related things happened.

From a few — but not all — of the legionnaires there rose a dull, inarticulate rumble of protest. Like the groan of a protesting piece of machinery.

From Taeti came a speech.

It was a largely indistinct speech, emerging from his smashed face. It was gabbled and hysterical. And it was addressed direct to the legionnaires.

Taeti turned towards them. Still holding his face with one hand, he gestured wildly with the other

'He's the murderer . . . Laubert's the murderer . . . didn't he drive Zicco to suicide . . . ? Wasn't he wanting to kill . . . to kill Katz . . . ?'

He broke off. Horfal made a move towards him, but Laubert gestured him back. Laubert was watching the Hawaiian with interest. And with a faint suggestion of amusement.

'I was saying . . . Katz . . . he was wanting to kill him . . . he'll kill us all . . . mad

73

. . . that's what he is . . . the lieutenant wanted to arrest him . . . isn't that proof? . . . We all heard about the lieutenant . . . he isn't fit to command us . . . if you let him kill me, he'll kill you . . . get rid of him . . . shoot him . . . *shoot Laubert* . . . '

With his final appeal, Taeti collapsed on his back. He lay there in a swoon.

The column gazed upon his inert form. The column in this moment was devoid of human personality. Just a line of transfixed countenances.

If Laubert had not been impelled by his dark heart . . .

If Laubert had used a mere modicum of discretion . . .

If Laubert had not drawn his pistol . . . If . . .

But Laubert took the very course which was calculated to destroy discipline. Even after Taeti had spoken, the legionnaires remained a coherent military body. Their hatred of Laubert had not lessened their automatic capacity for obeying orders. In a vague way, most of them sympathised with Taeti while recognising that an attempt to shoot an officer in the back was an intolerable action. They were still under the influence of the most rigid military training on earth.

Until Laubert pulled out his pistol and aimed it at Taeti.

That was too much. The calculated butchery of an unconscious man was something few of them could stomach. Particularly when it was presented as an act of military law.

Laubert was balancing the pistol in his hand when the column broke formation. They moved between Laubert and Taeti.

They did so silently. Menacingly. Slowly. Like the advance of a wave of oil.

Horfal shouted an order. No one knew what it was. No one cared. It was ignored.

Within a few seconds nearly fifty legionnaires had halted in a disordered mass around the senseless man. All of them were watching Laubert.

And suddenly Laubert was frightened. Which was natural. But he showed his fear. Which was bad.

He waved his pistol, his eyes wild. Then he turned to Horfal and shouted: 'Sergeant! Give the order resume column of march immediately.'

It was a clear announcement that he did not trust himself to give the order.

Horfal braced himself. He did his best. He called the commands as he would have done on a parade ground — as if he did not doubt they would be obeyed. But the result was nil. The silent men remained where they were.

There are times when a man wonders whether some outstandingly ghastly experience is real. He hopes it is not, while deep within him knowing that it is. Horfal was experiencing that emotion.

Never in his long years as a soldier had he endured anything remotely like this. He took the only possible course. He decided to forget his rank and make a direct appeal to the legionnaires.

'Listen to me!' he shouted. 'Do you forget that we are under orders to reach the town of Baikas? Do you forget that people are waiting for us there . . . waiting for us to protect them? There is only one . . . '

'That will be enough, Sergeant Horfal.'

Laubert had cut in. Laubert, it seemed,

had recovered his nerve.

In comparison to Horfal, he spoke quietly to the legionnaires. He said: 'I am ordered to reach Baikas. Therefore I will reach Baikas. I will take with me those men who obey the command to reform column of march. The others will return to the fort. They will be dealt with under military usage.'

None moved.

Then, from somewhere in the midst of the mass of men, a voice asked in debased French: 'What about Taeti?'

'Legionnaire Taeti is under sentence of death. I will carry it out myself.'

Suddenly there was a new surge of sound as all the legionnaires seemed to talk at the same time. Some tried to address themselves to Laubert and Horfal. Others spoke among themselves. Laubert opened his mouth as if to shout above the row. But Horfal put a restraining hand on his elbow.

'Please, *mon officier*, leave them . . . '

Laubert took the advice. It was probably the only sensible thing he had done since leaving the fort. His every other act had been a miscalculation.

And, gradually, a rough pattern of order emerged from the chaos. Some of the legionnaires remained around Taeti. Some formed again into a column.

When Horfal made a rough count, he saw that the new column was composed of less than half the strength. About twenty men. He noted that Legionnaire Katz was among them. And Legionnaire Sayle was next to him.

And the others . . .

They had picked up Taeti. The Hawaiian was conscious again, but he could stand only with assistance. Several men were whispering to him. He hissed something back.

Laubert saw this. He shouted: 'Legionnaire Taeti is to remain here.'

It was an ill-considered command. But Laubert was confronted with a situation for which there was probably no precedent. His words were greeted with a round of unsubdued oaths. And some mirthless laughter.

Leaning on the shoulders of two men, Taeti emerged from the mob. Despite his cruel injuries, despite his weakness, he was triumphant. He had his followers. This was Taeti's moment.

He produced a semi-distinct shout. He said: 'I am not staying here, *capitaine*! And we're not going back to the fort . . . not to wait for an execution squad! We're deserting . . . all of us! We're not going to die . . . '

But he did die. He died at that precise second.

His already mauled face was finally shattered by rifle bullet. It was one of several.

A volley of shots was being aimed into their midst.

It was a carefully-aimed, controlled volley. It ripped gaps into the living wall of legionnaires. Where men had been standing, suddenly men were sprawling.

The volley was fired by a line of men who were strung on the summit of some dunes, six hundred yards to the east.

Laubert and Horfal saw them at the same time. They saw the brown faces in unfamiliar grey uniforms.

And Laubert said: '*Dieu!* They look like soldiers! Like Arab soldiers!'

5

Minor Engagement

It took Laubert only a few moments to get over the initial shock. Then he acted according to instinct and training. It was in just such a situation as this that he was at his best.

He groped in the breast-pocket of his tunic, extracted his whistle. On it he blew three short blasts — the Standing Emergency Order to take cover.

Most of the legionnaires had thrown themselves on the sand before the second volley was fired from the dunes. But a few, slower than the others, were hit in the upper parts of the body as they flung themselves forward.

Deliberately, Laubert remained on his feet for the better part of half a minute. It was not bravado. He wanted to obtain a clear impression of the tactical situation. Horfal stood with him.

It was obvious that these soldiers had advanced from the east and taken up their position on and slightly behind the dunes while chaos had reigned in the Legion ranks.

Laubert said: 'How many, do you think?'

'A hundred, *mon capitaine*.'

'I agree. We are lucky they did not come closer. Get down!'

They dropped flat just before the third volley. This time little damage was done. The legionnaires had dispersed into a wide semi-circle. Most of the bullets passed over their heads or bored into the soft ground.

But so far there had been no return fire. No order had been given. The legionnaires waited. They were transformed in the face of danger. They were once more a highly-disciplined force.

Laubert said: 'We must tempt them forward. I must have prisoners — wounded or otherwise. I want to know who these people are.'

Horfal nodded. He said: 'We hold our fire?'

'We do a little better than that. We try to make them believe that we have suffered very great casualties, that there is only a handful left among us. That will induce them to attack. Sergeant Horfal . . . choose five men. Tell them to fire wildly.'

Horfal crawled away. He cursed as he did so. Cursed Laubert. *Tiens!* Why did he have to be such a superb soldier? If only he were incompetent! It was wrong. It was unsettling, that a cruel maniac should possess this virtue. But that was life, he told himself as he edged forward. The bad were seldom wholly bad.

He reached Legionnaire Sayle first. The Englishman had scooped for himself a primitive foxhole. He was toying with the bolt of his Lebel. There was an expression of sardonic interest on his finely-cut, intellectual face. He nodded to Horfal.

'We have visitors,' he said.

The Englishman's sense of humour was beyond the Spaniard's comprehension. It occurred to Horfal that in his experience most Englishmen made fantastic and senseless remarks when faced with danger.

'Listen, legionnaire. Allow two minutes, then shoot at those swine. But don't shoot too well.'

Sayle raised one eyebrow — a quizzical trick of his.

'I don't understand. Why?'

It was a clear case where men must understand the reason for orders in order to carry them out properly.

Horfal explained.

Sayle nodded again. He looked thoughtful.

'And is this . . . is this Captain Laubert's plan?'

'It is. He wants prisoners. He must know what's happening.'

As he turned to crawl to the next man, Horfal caught a deepening expression of puzzlement on Sayle's face

He knew how Sayle felt. He felt the same way. This Laubert was an enigma . . .

There was little fire now from the Arab troops. They must be watching, trying to assess the damage they had inflicted.

And there was plenty of evidence of that damage. Horfal counted eleven very still bodies, which certainly would never move again. There was something abstract about them. They merely looked like so many pieces of contorted material. As if they had never really existed. It was not the first time that Horfal had thought that there was nothing dramatic, nothing moving, even, about sudden death. It was just the supreme anti-climax. But that was not so of the wounded. He saw that sixteen or seventeen men had suffered wounds. Most of them were slight, and they were dressing them themselves from their aid packs. But three men were dying. One of them was sobbing while a comrade tried in a crude way to help him. Horfal shuddered. He hated to hear men weep. It seemed vaguely indecent . . .

Legionnaire Katz was the next man to receive the order to fire. He was stretched out with his rifle trained on the distant dunes. His mobile face expressed astonishment as Horfal spoke.

'Fire wildly!' Katz repeated when Horfal finished. 'It is not natural!'

But after Horfal had explained, he said: 'It is a clever plan. It has a touch of genius. Captain Laubert . . . he must be a master tactician.'

As he crawled away, Horfal marvelled at the Austrian's words. Horfal suspected that Katz was too big a man to indulge in hatreds.

He got back to Laubert. The captain had his field glasses trained on the dunes. He continued to look through them as he said: 'All arranged, sergeant? They understand?'

'*Oui, capitaine.* I have spoken to the five men myself. Word is being passed to the others to keep very still.'

'I have only one worry.'

'And that, *capitaine?*'

'I fear they may not be deceived. They can see us better than we can see them, for they are at a higher altitude. They may know that we have not suffered very great casualties. What are our casualties?'

Horfal told him.

Laubert lowered his glasses. He said: 'It's worse than I thought . . . and we have to reach Baikas! But first we must identify these soldiers . . . *Dieu!* Who can they be? We must get the prisoners. Only they can give us the answer . . . '

At that moment Sayle opened fire.

It was an excellent simulation of panic. He discharged three shots with the frantic rapidity of a frightened man.

After a short pause, Katz followed. Then the three others. The rest, save for the contortions of the severely wounded, stayed prone.

There was an answering volley from the dunes. It showed impressive fire discipline, beginning and ending with crisp precision. But the column was under good cover. Those who had not scooped themselves foxholes were behind large stones and rocks, which are a plentiful feature of the Algerian desert. There was only one additional casualty — a legionnaire lost the tip of a thumb.

Horfal called an order.

After a pause, only three legionnaires fired. It was a thin volley in comparison to that from the dunes.

Then a pause of two long, heavy minutes.

Laubert watched again through his glasses. The rest stared with unassisted eyes.

They saw movement. A tentative, uncertain movement. Like the first uncoiling of a waking snake. And suddenly the strange, grey-clad soldiers were on their feet, silhouettes against the sky. They stood thus for several moments.

Laubert hissed: 'Keep still . . . they're watching us.'

Later, Horfal whispered: 'They're coming, *capitaine*!'

They were advancing in open order, widely spaced. It was now easy to see that the original guess at their strength had been roughly correct. There were about ninety of them. Their uniforms were curious. The tunics and breeches were of western cut. And there was nothing oriental about their equipment. But, by contrast, each head was swathed in a white Arabic tarboosh.

It was a slow, meticulous advance. And soon it became apparent that it was a skilful one. The centre of the line was hanging back while each flank made an encircling movement.

Horfal said: 'They're going to form a ring round us before they close in.'

Laubert answered with a mumbled oath. He knew that the unexpected Arab deployment placed him in a critical situation. The legionnaires, feigning death could not move to face the ring that was forming round them. Not unless they revealed the deception prematurely. But if they waited . . . If they waited they would be butchered before they could fire a shot.

There was only one answer — to open fire before the encircling movement could take full effect. This meant that the Arabs on the flanks were about four hundred yards off; the middle of the line a good five hundred yards. Not as close as Laubert had planned. But they would still have the advantage of surprise. And they would certainly inflict many casualties. It was casualties that Laubert wanted — wounded casualties who would talk.

Laubert raised himself very slightly on his elbows. He surveyed the prone legionnaires around him.

He pitched his voice so his words carried to all of them, but not to the approaching Arabs.

'When I give a single whistle blast you

open fire,' he said. 'Five rounds rapid — no more. Then reload.'

There was no movement from the great majority of the legionnaires. They were playing their part well. Even at close quarters they looked like corpses. Those who were not already corpses.

Laubert wasted another minute. Until the Arab flanks were parallel with his own. Then he put the whistle between his discoloured teeth and blew.

The result appeared as a combination of movement and sound. More than thirty legionnaires (including the slightly wounded) suddenly grabbed their Lebels. There was scarcely a detectable interval before they fired, some from their prone positions, some kneeling.

The five rounds were released in something under seven seconds. And they were devastatingly accurate rounds.

The Arabs, believing that they were approaching an utterly shattered column, were momentarily paralysed. They stopped at the first movement of the legionnaires. They remained still and abject targets. They suffered accordingly.

When the final shot had been fired, rather more than two-thirds of their number were sprawled on the sand. The rest — mostly those who had been in the centre and therefore at the greatest distance from the legionnaires — were turning to run.

Horfal and Laubert watched anxiously as the men reloaded.

The menace from the Arabs was broken. Completely broken. But it was obviously desirable to prevent any escaping, if that was possible. It became a race between the fleeing Arabs and the fingers of the legionnaires. The Arabs won. Aided by the speed of fear, they had a great advantage. If the column had been equipped with British Lee Enfields or German Mausers they would have been able to fire again before the Arabs were out of range. But the French Lebel took three times as long to load as either of those other types of rifle.

Laubert shouted: 'Let them go — you can't reach them.'

Then he said to Horfal: 'Now we will look at these Arab soldiers. Perhaps will discover who they are and what they are doing in French territory.'

Eighteen of the Arabs still lived. Thirteen of them were in a fit condition to be hauled to their feet and paraded in front of Laubert.

Laubert walked down the short line, looking at them with intense curiosity. They were, in some respects, less impressive at close quarters. Those grey uniforms, for example, were ill-fitting. No self-respecting western army would have equipped men like that. And Laubert was astounded to see that they wore boots. Poor quality and well-worn boots. But boots, none the less. Which was most unusual — and probably highly uncomfortable — apparel for Arabs.

And their equipment, which had looked highly efficient from a distance, was revealed as an odd assortment. The rifles that lay at their feet were modern enough. But they were not standardised. Some were Polish, coming out of the Skoz works. A couple were American Springfields. The others were of unidentifiable manufacture. The only thing they had in common was the fact that they used the same .30C ammunition.

Their cartridge pouches were similarly varied. Some were British — of the type that had been in service up to the outbreak of the Second World War. Others were German.

But the men themselves . . .

There was nothing to sneer at there.

Despite their wounds, despite their captivity, they carried themselves proudly. Almost arrogantly. They had the air of men who are disciplined and glad of the fact. None of them showed any fear as Laubert stared into their faces.

Laubert finally fixed his attention on one man whose uniform differed from the others in that it carried what seemed to be badges of rank on the sleeves. He had a wrist wound.

Speaking in slow French, Laubert said: 'I require to know who you are and where you come from. Also why you have fired at us.'

The Arab did not appear to hear. He was a tallish man, and he continued to stare indifferently into the middle distance.

Laubert repeated the question. Still no answer.

Horfal suggested: 'Perhaps he does not understand French.'

'Perhaps not — but I think he does. I'll try Arabic.'

Laubert's Arabic met the minimum requirements of a Legion officer. It was hesitant, fumbling. But it was understandable. He phrased the question in that tongue.

Again the Arab remained unmoved.

By now Laubert's fleshy face was colouring. And there was glitter of hard malice in his eyes.

He said: 'We'll try new methods. Methods they will understand. Sergeant Horfal — choose one of the others. Any of them will do. And shoot him. I think that will persuade our dumb friend that I am serious.'

Horfal hesitated. In his time he had killed many men, but not defenceless men.

'Do as I order, sergeant!'

'Could we not . . . '

'Shoot!'

Horfal shrugged. He obeyed the order because he had no alternative. And because he realised the urgent necessity of getting the information from the Arabs.

He unslung his rifle. He did not cause unnecessary suffering by going through a hideously obvious process of selection. With a single tossing movement he brought his Lebel to his shoulder and fired at the Arab on the extreme left of the line. It was probably over before the man knew he had been condemned.

The Arab himself turned a grotesque backward somersault before lying still on his belly.

That broke the stoic resistance. It shattered the arrogance. The Arabs turned, looked with frightened eyes at the remains.

Laubert did not give them a chance to recover. He again confronted the tall Arab. Reverting to French, he said: 'You will give me the information I want, or I will kill each of you in turn. I will save you to the end.'

There was a caressing, loving intonation to Laubert's voice. The voice of a man who enjoyed the prospective torture.

The Arab said: 'I will tell you what you want to know.'

His French was moderately fluent. He was suddenly very afraid. It was obvious that he had expected to receive orthodox military treatment. He had not anticipated a brutality which was probably the equal of his own.

Laubert smiled thinly. 'If you'd said that before, you would have saved a life. Now tell me about yourselves. And I warn you — no lies.'

'We are soldiers of the Hanah republic.'

Several of the legionnaires who comprehended the significance of the answer gave involuntary sighs of astonishment. Laubert rubbed his soft chin.

'Then you have infringed French territorial rights. You are miles over the border. And you have fired on French troops. That is an act of war. Why have you done this?'

'Because you are about to invade our territory.'

'*Dieu!* Invade with a handful of men! This is absurd!'

'You were moving towards our borders. Others will follow you. You will take advantage of the blood shed in my country to place it again under French bondage.'

'You speak nonsense! I can ... ' Laubert broke off as the blatant question occurred to him. He grasped the Arab's badly-fitting tunic. He said: 'How did you know we were moving on Hanah? Tell me that — if you want to live!'

The Arab glanced at the others. He said: 'If I do not tell you, the others will do so. We are men of courage, but we do not want to die ... so you will learn of the strange events in my land of Hanah ... '

$$\star \quad \star \quad \star$$

For years Hanah had been like a kettle just off the boil. It had simmered, it had grumbled, under the republican regime which had taken over when it was granted independence.

There was nothing new, nothing outstandingly dramatic about the internal troubles of that country. It simply arose out of the fact that a small minority of comparatively intelligent people held power, which they used harshly and corruptly, exploiting the great mass or illiterate or semi-literate inhabitants. If the French occupation of the territory had been a tyranny, the new self-governing regime was no better. The only difference was that a competent western administration had been replaced by an incompetent Arabic one.

The new regime was Republican only in name. In fact, it was an Autocracy of shrewd and merciless men who grew fat on the taxes they imposed on a sullen population.

Hanah — like many Arab territories — had always been divided by deep hatreds. But never so much as now.

Yet the government under the presidency of Bav Usta had been confident that Hanah's small standing army could always deal with any attempted rising. For the army was well treated. And (by Arab standards) it was well equipped with a miscellany of unwanted material that had been purchased from munitions dumps soon after the end of the Second World War.

But the unexpected happened.

Fully half of the army had mutinied

against the regime. And they had seized control of almost all the country, except Baikas the capital. In Baikas, the insurgents had been able to capture and to hold only the radio station and a few minor official buildings around it.

The result had been planned as strictly a military affair. But such matters seldom go according to plan. This was no exception.

The mobs took control.

Having been shown the way, they rose hideous in their fury. No mob is so terrible as an Arab mob. These ran true to tradition. They pillaged, they burned, under the pretence of seeking justice. Scarcely a village, scarcely a home save those of the most humble, was untouched by them. For the agitators who led them were even less scrupulous than the men they sought to overthrow.

Even the insurgent soldiers who attempted to stop the worst of their excesses were themselves attacked.

So Hanah's divided army became united again. It had to — for self-preservation.

And Baikas was the last place where

they held nominal control. The mobs there had looted the homes of the French civilians. They had seized — and wrecked — the silver mines. They dominated most of the squalid streets.

Only the government buildings stayed out of their blood-stained hands. The government buildings and the French legation — the only legation in Baikas.

Within the area skulked a trembling government. And two-score French nationals. They were protected by a thin ring of Arab troops. But the troops, their own nerve badly shaken, could not for long hold out against the mob pressure.

That was the situation in Hanah when the radio station at Baikas picked up the French legation's radio plea for protection. The replies from Paris and Bel Abbes were missed, because the receiver was of poor quality. But the officers of the Hanah army had heard enough.

Clearly, it was argued, the French would use this excuse to re-occupy the country. And they would again find themselves a French protectorate.

Anything was better than that.

Then the President, Bav Usta, saw that here was a way of escape. Here was the means by which he might save his own skin and unite the entire country behind him.

He had only to convince the mob that a French invading force was on the way, then every man, woman and child in Hanah would rally in defence of their frontiers.

But first some definite evidence of the approach of French forces must be provided.

Bav Usta was no fool. He saw immediately that — since the country was too remote and physically unsuitable for air operations — the French must make their first move from the nearby Fort Iama.

An advance force, Bav Usta argued, would come from that fort. Others would follow.

And so . . .

Nearly a hundred men, under the command of an intrepid officer named Yssan, were immediately moved under the cover of night out of Baikas. They were under orders to intercept the Legion column, engage it briefly, then withdraw with all speed back to Baikas. And there they were to make the sensational report which would rally and unite the mobs. A report which would turn their fury away from their government . . .

★   ★   ★

That was the story that Yssan told.

He told it tersely, and his words had the clear ring of truth. When Yssan had done, Laubert mopped his brow. He said: 'You were fortunate to catch us unawares. If you had not done so, you'd never have inflicted casualties upon us. As it is — I thank you for your information. You will be escorted to Fort Iama.'

Yssan looked worried.

'And what is to become of us?'

'You will be held prisoners to await my return. Then I will seek sanction for your execution. When I receive it, I will supervise the ceremony myself.'

Yssan hesitated. He was puzzled. Then: 'You must get permission to slay us?'

'I must.'

'Then you broke your own laws by slaying one of my men when he was your prisoner.'

Laubert laughed. Not a pleasant laugh. 'He should not have attempted to escape.'

'Escape! He was standing here when he was shot . . . '

'*Non, mon ami*. He was running away. I remember it quite well. I called him back, but the stupid fellow ran on. I will explain it all in my report.'

The Arab's body became taut, like a stretching rope.

He sprang at Laubert. His strong hands closed round Laubert's big neck.

But he had no chance to exert pressure before Horfal slapped the butt of his rifle against his kidneys. The Arab groaned and staggered back.

Laubert rubbed his throat. He switched a quick glance at Horfal.

'This is the second time you have saved me within an hour,' he said. 'I appreciate such loyalty.'

Laubert turned towards the distant fort. Only the limp Tricolour and the top of the observation tower showed over the horizon.

But presently, through his glasses, he saw a tiny column of about two dozen legionnaires approaching. They were headed by Lieutenant Du Pois. A very worried Du Pois, it became apparent. When he was still a mile away Laubert could see the strained desperation clearly on his face.

He lowered his glasses, said to Yssan: 'Your escort is arriving. For the time being you will be in the charge of a very ambitious young officer . . . is that not so, Sergeant Horfal?'

Horfal did not answer.

★   ★   ★

Du Pois almost vomited. The unlovely spectacle of the dead and the dying, spread over a wide perimeter, revolted his unhardened stomach. It was some time before he could react to Laubert's brief explanation.

Finally he said, hoarsely: 'The men who were going to desert . . . what will we do?'

'We will do nothing. Now they know what faces them, I think they will be glad to forget such ideas. *I* will remember — but later.'

'But are you sure you can rely on them?'

'I am certain of it. They are disloyal scum, but they are not cowards. They will not run away now they know that action is possible — even probable. In a sense, the Arabs have done me a favour.'

'*Oui* . . . but your strength has been terribly weakened. How many fit men have you?'

'Thirty-five.'

'*Tiens!* Thirty-five men to enter a hostile country. It was bad enough before, but now it is impossible!'

Laubert clenched his fists. Du Pois saw again the flicker of madness in his eyes. 'I do not deal in impossibilities, lieutenant! I do not even acknowledge that they exist. I am under orders to reach the capital town of Baikas — and I shall reach Baikas. I am under orders to protect French lives and property there — I shall protect French lives and property.'

He had spoken in a harsh undertone, so that only Du Pois heard. The lieutenant made a timid gesture towards the legionnaires he had brought with him.

'Then would it not be best to make up your strength from these men?'

'*Non*. The fort is already far below the minimum efficient strength. And this whole area may become infected with unrest because of what is happening in Hanah. So I cannot risk depleting the garrison further . . .'

Laubert paused to glance at the sun. The bottom edge was touching the horizon. He added: 'Time has been wasted. Vital time. My schedule allowed me twenty-four hours to reach Baikas. We will reach it in eighteen hours by increasing the marching pace and halving the rest periods. You can expect a radio signal from me when I reach the legation . . .'

6

The Englishman

Midnight. An uneasy hour.

The column had halted under a moon which was almost full. The silvery beam seemed to bleach the faces of the legionnaires. They had a vaguely unreal aspect. An ethereal transparency, a fragile lack of substance. Each face was a ghost face.

And the night wind had an icy touch. It breathed over the sand, it whispered with the bending clumps of cactus and camel thorn. It searched through each man's *capote* and *bougeron* so that they shivered.

This was not one of the infrequent rest periods. Not officially. It was a pause while Laubert, chart unrolled on the ground, compass and dividers to hand, made a dead reckoning calculation to establish that they had just crossed the south-south-western border of the state of Hanah.

A few legionnaires mumbled trite remarks to each other. But most were too weary, too tense for talk. It was easier to think.

Those who had threatened to desert the column, for example . . .

They were silent. They wondered whether, by a military miracle, they might escape court-martial.

And they shared a feeling that such a miracle might occur.

After all, they told themselves, Laubert was obviously mad. Had the lieutenant himself not threatened to put Laubert under arrest?

True, *le capitaine* was no fool. He had shown that when they were surprised by the Arabs. And that was good to know now that they were facing real danger. But the regrettable fact remained that the man who was no fool in a military action was also crazy when things were quiet.

So (they reasoned) perhaps there would not be a court-martial. Not after the lieutenant and the medical officer had made their report.

Others allowed their minds to dwell on different things. On matters which were remote from the Legion and yet part of it.

Take this man Brian Sayle . . .

His slim, taut figure was leaning slightly forward as he rested part of his weight on the muzzle of his Lebel. His mind was back in time.

Back to the woman he hated . . .

★   ★   ★

She had said to him: 'You need me, Brian. Why make yourself miserable? Let's get married.'

He had tried to argue. But it was always difficult to argue with Deidre. She had the type of feminine mind which is capable of comprehending only her own point of view.

'I haven't much money,' he said. 'I'm not earning much, and my savings are going.'

She pressed her dark head against his shoulders. Then he felt the contact of her sensual body. She linked her arms round his neck.

'But Brian, you will make a lot of money.

Clever barristers like you make fortunes.'

He had to smile. It was a typical misconception.

How could he convince her that — clever or not — as a newly-qualified and unknown member of the legal bar he might exist for years with scarcely a brief? He might have to calculate each day whether he could afford to buy a newspaper, as so many others had done.

The public thought of the legal profession as being exclusively filled with suave and prosperous men. In fact, most of its members lived austere lives. And some tasted downright penury. Only the most gifted achieved the vast incomes which made headlines in the press.

He had decided to read for the bar when he left the army after six years' war service. He was demobilised with the rank of major (acting lieutenant-colonel), which meant that he received a gratuity of several hundred pounds. In addition, he had saved most of his pay.

And the government was prepared to help him qualify by providing special grants to cover part of the costs of training.

It seemed to be a chance worth taking. For, when the war ended, he was still only in his mid-twenties. And the law had always appealed to him as a career.

He knew that he possessed an incisive, logical mind. A mind which was naturally attracted to the close reasoning of legal argument.

And he had a basic belief in the importance of the rule of law. To Brian Sayle, good lawyers were more important to the community than good doctors. For without impartial justice no real civilisation could survive.

He qualified in the minimum three years and became a member of the Middle Temple.

There he went into chambers with a moderately-successful Q.C. He did a great deal of hard work for this eminent gentleman. For it he received no payment. He was lucky to be allowed to gather the experience. Perhaps, one day in the remote future, a solicitor would toss him a brief, he would earn a few guineas in court, then the money would start to roll in . . .

That was his hope. That was his intention.

And now Deidre wanted to get married.

How long had he known her?

Only a few months. He had been introduced to her when he was an unwilling guest at a cocktail party. She had an overpowering personality, had Deidre. She had fastened herself to Brian at that party and she had scarcely left him since. Not that he minded. She was attractive. And it was rather flattering.

Her arms gripped tightly round his neck.

Her brown eyes were looking hard into his. There was just a suggestion of brittleness about her. Brian had not noticed it before. It was a faint atmosphere of harsh calculation. It disturbed him.

She said slowly: 'Darling, you don't seem to understand . . . I *have* to get married . . . '

It was a lie.

He found that out a few weeks after their register office wedding.

He found out other things about her, too.

She was a spendthrift. She opened

accounts in his name at expensive shops. The first he knew about them was when he received the staggering bills.

She had the temper of a wildcat; she could use the invective of a bargee.

She made no serious attempt to look after the small flat they had taken in South Kensington. Except for her personal appearance, she was slovenly.

In short, Brian Sayle had caught a tartar. Or rather, a tartar had caught him.

They had been married six months when she was accused of shoplifting. She did not say anything to him about it. The first Brian knew of the matter was when he received an urgent call to a magistrate's court.

It all seemed unreal, in that court. There was a sense of fantasy in seeing Deidre in the dock with a policewoman at her side. She looked arrogantly at him.

The magistrate was most sympathetic. He said he had called Brian to see if he wished to give evidence for the defence.

'Your wife,' he said, 'has pleaded guilty to this particular charge. She has asked me to take some twenty similar charges into consideration when deciding the sentence . . . '

He paused, rustled with some cards, then continued: 'When she was only sixteen she was committed to an approved school because of thieving. Latterly, she has been fined various sums for obtaining credit by fraud, and there was also a case of common assault while drunk . . . '

The magistrate talked on. Brian listened in a sick daze. Finally, the figure on the bench said: 'If I commit her into your care in a surety of fifty pounds, will you see if you cannot use your influence to reform her?'

He said he would try.

They did not speak as they left the court together.

An hour later the evening newspapers were out. And when Brian saw the headlines he knew his legal career was finished.

Barrister's Wife Steals from Shop.

'I'll Try to Reform My Wife' — *Barrister Tells Court.*

And plenty of others in the same vein.

All the reports were accurate. All the headlines merely summarised the facts.

The newspapers were simply doing their job of giving the news.

But the English legal profession demanded the highest standards not only from its members, but also from those with whom its members associated.

He knew he could, if he wished, carry on. Fellow lawyers would be polite. They would pretend to ignore the whole unsavoury business. But really they would remember him as the man who had the wife who . . .

The public would remember, too. And they would not want to be represented by a barrister whose wife was a petty criminal.

Brian did not quarrel with those facts. He believed passionately in justice. Justice must be inflexible in the conduct it demanded of the people who administered it. He had only himself to blame if he had married a tramp . . .

A tramp! A clever tramp. That's all Deidre was.

For the fact was proven beyond doubt just a month later.

Brian had taken a job teaching French

and Latin at a night school. One night, while he was working, Deidre sold the furniture in their flat. It was removed in a van. She sold most of his clothes, too. Then she disappeared in a high-powered car with a flashily-dressed man who operated a dubious gambling business on the south coast.

All men have a breaking point. All men can reach a stage where they say 'Enough — I quit.'

But there are different ways of quitting.

Brian spent a night in a pub getting very drunk before he decided the path he would take.

He wanted to find a place of escape. An occupation where he was not called upon to think over much. Where an entirely different atmosphere would not remind him of a life in shambles.

Soldiering was the logical answer.

Having spent six years as a war-time soldier, he knew that he fitted tolerably well into the military atmosphere. He found that it had its drawbacks — the greatest being the almost complete loss of liberty. But it had its compensations, too.

But where was he to do his soldiering?

His first instinct was to rejoin the British army. But he soon realised that there were snags to this plan. Because he was an ex-officer who had been indirectly involved in a scandal, the War Office might be reluctant to renew his commission. He would have joined the ranks. But again the fact that he had been an officer stood in the way. No doubt he would ultimately be accepted as a private soldier — but not until many very tedious formalities had been completed. And these might take months.

He was not willing to wait months.

Then he remembered the French Foreign Legion.

During the war, while in the Middle East, he had been temporarily billeted near a Legion detachment. Like all the others in his unit, he had regarded the legionnaires with great curiosity. It had been exciting to see in the flesh these soldiers whose battle prowess had so caught the world's imagination.

He was surprised by what he saw. But not disappointed.

He soon discovered that the Legion no longer consisted exclusively of thugs and misfits. There was a proportion of these, of course, but not many.

Many of the legionnaires were victims of racial or political persecution, who enlisted to lead a life of honourable self-respect. A few were professional adventurers who found that this international army satisfied their craving for excitement. And some (perhaps most) were just men who had never had a chance to achieve anything in their own country. Not victims of injustice. Not men hiding any personal tragedy. Simply men who had never had a fair shake. Under the Tricolour they found what they wanted.

All of them found what they wanted. For the Legion did not care a jot about the pigmentation of a man's skin. It had no interest in his religious beliefs beyond allowing him freedom to practise them. It judged a man only on what was in his heart.

During that first brief war-time contact with the Legion, Brian discovered, too, that the Legion had an immense pride in its reputation as a fighting force. A pride which was not even surpassed by the British Brigade of Guards.

So the Legion was the place. The Legion offered escape. He took a week-end ticket from Dover and enlisted in Boulogne.

And he found forgetfulness. He was almost happy.

Until he was mustered into a company commanded by Captain Laubert. And posted to Fort Iama.

Laubert epitomised everything he hated.

The glaring sensuality. The cunning sadism. They revolted a man who, by his earlier training, had a precise idea of justice. Not that Laubert and he had crossed swords personally. But Brian had simmered over the events which led to the suicide of Zicco.

And he had been on the point of mutiny when his friend Katz was threatened.

For he had formed an immediate friendship with the quiet, brave little Jew.

If the difference in rank had not separated him, he would probably have made a friend of Sergeant Horfal, too. He liked the Spaniard's honest simplicity. And he realised that Horfal was in a desperate position now — torn between loyalty to his officer and a justifiable revulsion against him.

Legionnaire Brian Sayle, once a junior barrister, leaned on his rifle and brooded on . . .

* * *

Laubert rolled the chart, inserted it in a leather case. He pushed his dividers and compass into his breast pocket. He turned towards the column and called: '*Regardez!*'

The few who had been talking suddenly became silent.

The others ceased to dream. The shadows of the past dissolved under the impact of Laubert's voice.

Laubert spoke briskly, in the manner of a man who was compelled to give an explanation but did not wish to take long over it.

He said: 'We are now about three miles inside the territory of Hanah. Now remember this — we have not come here to seek a fight with anyone. Our task is to protect the civilians in the legation at Baikas . . . '

He paused only long enough to give emphasis, then added: 'But I fear we may meet trouble before we reach the legation, which is another eight hours' hard marching from here. You heard from our prisoners that the government of Hanah is encouraging the belief that we are about to re-occupy the country so as to divert the fury of the mob against us . . .

'Word of our approach will already have reached the people here through the Arabs who survived the action. We must be ready for attempts to obstruct our march to Baikas. But I do not think it will be organised obstruction. There will not be time for that. It will probably be no more than minor attacks from misguided bands of Arabs. Now be clear in your minds — we will avoid action if we possibly can. Nothing must delay our arrival in Baikas. For that reason, I am sending ahead an advance patrol of two men, who will report any sign of Arab activity on our route.'

He went through the gesture of licking his fat lips. Then: 'Legionnaires Katz and Sayle — three paces forward, march!'

Brian was a fraction slow in obeying the order because it was entirely unexpected. He was slightly behind Katz as they stamped forward and came to attention in front of Laubert.

'*Repos!*'

They stood easy again.

Laubert said more slowly: 'You two will assume the scouting duty. I have chosen you because I gather you are both men of initiative.'

There was no suggestion of sarcasm in the vocal inflexions. In fact, he spoke as if offering a slight compliment. But Brian Sayle was looking into his eyes. Under the moon, they were glinting blobs of evil. He was obviously amused by his own choice.

Laubert continued in amicable tones: 'The route from here to Baikas is due south-east. But you will not need a compass. Within a mile of here there is a secondary military road which the Legion built when this place was a French protectorate. It takes us to Baikas, and we will use it.

'You will move four hundred yards ahead of the column. Is that understood?'

'*Oui, capitaine.*'

'If you see anything which may obstruct us, one of you will report back to me. Don't make any fuss. Avoid noise. Try not to be seen. Only fire warning shots if you have no choice. I want to move round the Arabs — not fight through them. Any questions?'

Katz said quietly: 'There's some vegetation here, *mon capitaine*. Does that mean we're moving out of the desert region?'

Laubert nodded. 'It does. As we get nearer Baikas we'll find we are in scrubland. It is not dense, but it may give cover to the Arabs. Take care.'

They had taken a bearing from a star. And they moved south-east to where they were due to come upon the military road. At first they did not speak. They listened to their boots crunching against the sand. For they felt very alone, even though the column was a mere four hundred yards behind.

After half an hour they saw ahead, and

at the bottom of a slight declivity, what seemed to be a thin, dirty ribbon laid upon the rocky ground.

Katz said: 'That's it! That's the road.'

It felt good to stand upon that road. Suddenly the atmosphere seemed less primitive. Less menacing. It was like making a contact with civilisation.

But a civilisation of long ago.

For in the years since the Legion had withdrawn from Hanah, that road had fallen into neglect. The surface had cracked under heat and cold. Much of it was covered by a thick layer of sand.

Here in the moonlight, visibility was good. Only the dunes gave cover for a surprise assault. But these were becoming less numerous as sand gave way to rock and camel thorn.

Brian said in an undertone: 'I don't like this. I know someone's got to do the job, but I'd rather it wasn't me.'

Katz chuckled.

'I expected it. Laubert had to send scouts ahead of the column. Therefore I knew I'd be one of them.'

He sounded genuinely amused. The

little Austrian's French was guttural, but he injected a wealth of inflection into his phrases.

'You mean because . . . '

'Yes, because I was due to be the next object of his attention. He was frustrated. But he'll try to make up for it by giving me every unpleasant duty that comes along. I think it will be the same for you.'

'I don't see why, Katz. I haven't come to his notice in any special way.'

'But I think you have! You do not fear him, and you make the fact plain. He hates you for that. You know . . . I am disappointed in Captain Laubert.'

'Disappointed! Hell, I'd put it stronger than that!'

They trudged on for a few paces in silence.

Then Katz said: 'You don't understand me. You see, Laubert is mentally unbalanced because he's had months of isolation and no activity. That's obvious. I've seen such things happen before. But I hoped that he would become normal now that so much is happening — now that he has outlets for his energy. Yet, he's not normal. You can see that. He's still mad.'

Brian glanced in surprise at Katz. He said: 'You speak like an expert.'

'I studied psychiatry under Freud in Vienna until the Nazis came.'

'Well . . . couldn't you have gone on with your studies? Why the blazes are you in this army?'

'I think perhaps for the same reason as you, my friend. Things went very wrong.'

Obviously Katz did not wish to continue the topic. He regretted having asked the question.

'I'm sorry,' he said. 'I didn't . . . '

He broke off.

He heard a faint sound from far ahead. So did Katz. Both stopped in mid-stride, listening.

At first it was an indefinite pattering noise. But as it approached it became recognisable as the fall of feet on the road. Brian swiftly moved six paces to the left. Katz ran the same distance in the opposite direction. They lay flat on the ground so that they became all but invisible. They pulled their Lebel butts into their shoulders and stared over the leaf sights, waiting.

Brian thought in a confused way: 'They're light footsteps . . . and it sounds like only one man.'

Then, when perhaps three hundred yards ahead, the sound assumed physical substance. But only a vague substance. Just a single, indeterminate figure running down the centre of the narrow road. And running fast, robes spread out.

Brian hissed across to Katz: 'You keep still. Leave this to me.'

He heard Katz give a brief grunt of assent.

By now the figure was less than a hundred yards off. But Brian dared not take a clear look — if he raised his head too far he would certainly be seen. He waited, prone. Judging distance by sound alone. And, silently, he extracted his bayonet from its scabbard.

The quick, light steps were very near. He could hear heavy, strained breathing. The breathing of someone who is exhausted, but impelled by terror.

He waited until the figure was almost parallel with him.

Then his slim but well-muscled body

seemed to project itself upright like a released spring.

He had timed it well.

The shadowy figure was almost exactly level. He sprang across the intervening few yards, attacking from behind.

His left arm circled a throat, his elbow forcing up the chin so that no sound could be made. Retained impetus pulled him forward a few steps. When they stopped he pressed the bayonet against thin ribs.

Suddenly, he knew.

Knew it was a woman he was holding.

The body was so slight, so light. The chin which he was forcing so cruelly back was soft and smooth. He felt a dull sense of shock. Of vague indecency.

He lowered the bayonet, released the arm hold. He twisted her round so that she faced him. He thought: 'It'll be some Arab woman.'

But the terrified face which looked at him was white. And it was a lovely face, despite the distortion of fear. Despite the grime, which caked the skin and matted her long, fair hair.

For seconds they stared at each other.

She leaning against him. She parted her rich lips to speak. But at first no words came. Only a whimpering, panting sound.

Brian said in French: 'Take your time . . . you've nothing to be afraid of, now . . . '

They were weak, inadequate words. But he had to say something.

She tried again. This time she managed to articulate. And, even then, Brian felt a stab of astonishment. For her words came in a strange sort of French. The perversely-accented French that Arabs always used. Yet she was no Arab . . .

She whispered: 'Is it . . . is it that the Legion has come back to Hanah . . . ?'

Because she was swaying, he put an arm round her shoulders. But he did not answer the question. In stead, he asked: 'Who are you? What are you running away from?'

'*Je suis . . . Lydia . . .* '

'Very well — your name's Lydia. Now tell me the rest.'

She shook her head in a desperate gesture. Then she gazed, her blue eyes wide, over his shoulder in the direction from which she had come. Brian glanced round. There was nothing. Only Katz, who had moved beside them. A very startled, very puzzled Katz.

Abruptly, her small figure became tense. It was suddenly like thin whipcord in his arms. He knew the reason. He heard it with her. It was a steady, rhythmical tramping sound. The column coming up. He had forgotten about the column.

Brian tried to smile at her.

'You'll have to tell your story, whatever it is, to our captain,' he said. 'He is coming now.'

She twisted out of his supporting arms. She stood very still as the column gradually emerged out of the gloom. And when she saw them she turned back to Brian.

There were tears on her face. Her mouth was trembling.

'Are those all of your soldiers?' she asked in her strange French.

He nodded.

She gave a sob. A sob of abysmal despair.

'*Dieu!* So few of them! Too few! You will not live to see the daylight . . . '

7

The Forgotten Lady

Laubert listened with no more than detached interest while Brian made his report. His eyes were steady on the woman.

When Brian had finished, Laubert gave a brief nod.

They formed a strange spectacle, all of them on that derelict desert road. In the rear, the tiny column of legionnaires standing three abreast at ease. All watching the woman. Then, only slightly ahead, Laubert with Brian and Katz. They, too, were watching the woman.

And the woman . . .

She was a little apart from them all. And facing them. Very small, very slender. Still sobbing. But quietly.

Laubert cleared his throat. Then: 'You are obviously a European,' he said crisply. 'Am I right in thinking that you have somehow managed to get away from the French legation in Baikas?'

She looked at the ground, shook her head.

'I have come from Baikas — but I was not in the legation. Thank God I was not in that place! It was . . . '

Her words faded out in a choke of emotion.

Laubert rubbed the bristles on his fleshy jowl.

'We'll take things in order. First — your name and nationality, *s'il vous plait.*'

'My name is Lydia.'

'The legionnaire has told me that much. Now give me your other name. Are you French?'

'I have no other name — only Lydia. I am not French. I do not know which country I belong to . . . I do not think I belong to any . . . ' She made a small, desperate gesture. Then she added: 'I can explain, but there is not time now. We must get away from here! Get over the border . . . you understand? Out of Hanah! It's our only chance . . . '

She held out her arms to Laubert, as if

in supplication. Laubert decided to put the question which Brian had already asked without result.

'What are you afraid of?'

She looked again along the road and to each side of it. By instinct, all the others did the same. There was still nothing to be seen.

Then, facing Laubert again, she said in a voice which rose to almost a scream: 'It's the people! The people of Hanah are coming! They have risen in their thousands. And they are coming this way with a solemn oath on their lips. They say they will use the blood of the soldiers of France to . . . to enrich their dung piles! They swear that not one of the invaders will leave their land alive! They . . . '

'Be quiet!'

Laubert snapped the order at her viciously. It had to be admitted that he was right to do so. She was on the quivering verge of hysteria.

'You say they are coming this way,' Laubert continued. 'Have you seen them?'

'*Dieu, oui!* My friends gave me warning that they will kill all who have white skins. I saw them from far off before I fled, and they are as many as the grains of sand around us.'

Laubert was not impressed by the figuration. He said: 'And they are moving in this direction ... Very well, if they insist on trouble we will have to oblige them.'

She clenched her tiny fists.

'You do not understand! You are so few! You can do nothing. You must flee. They will be here soon!'

'And we will be here, too. I know how to deal with a mob, if I have to. And while we are waiting, you had better tell me about yourself. I require to know everything.'

For a moment she looked as if she was about to renew her protest. Then suddenly it was as if all the terror had left her. And utter resignation took its place. She shrugged her shoulders. Then, abruptly, she squatted down. It was a typically Arab posture. Assumed by a white woman, it was surprising.

She looked hard at Laubert. She said: 'I have nothing to hide, for I know very little about myself. But I will tell you what I do know . . . '

★   ★   ★

It was no more than a biological off-chance that Lydia was white. She remembered her mother, and she was a Parpatua Arab, the main sect in Hanah. She knew nothing of her father, save that he had been a German legionnaire during the time of the French occupation.

She was an outcast. The tiny white population of Hanah did not want her. The Arabs regarded her with suspicion.

Her home was among the hovels of Baikas. There, after her mother's death, she continued to earn a meagre existence making baskets to sell in the market.

Lydia — a name which had been bestowed upon her because it seemed suitably European — had been in Baikas when the Terror came.

Frightened, helpless, alone save for one or two Arabs who refused to be ashamed of her friendship, she saw the mobs take control of all except the administrative centre of the town.

She saw what had begun as an army revolt against a corrupt government turn into a ghastly orgy. Because of the white blood within her, she could not share in the wild hatred against the Europeans which had become a subsidiary chant of the mob. She felt sympathy and fear for the whites who had taken refuge in the French legation.

The day before, impelled by curiosity, she had gone into the town centre.

There, from a distance, she saw the massed thousands of inflamed and unthinking people who surrounded the legation and the buildings near it. People held back only by the thin lines of government soldiers.

It was as she watched that the first accusing fingers were pointed at her.

She was white! She was an enemy of the Arab people! She was an agent of the French . . .

Because she was on the fringe of the crowds, she was able to turn and flee. And, because she had not hesitated, she was able to shake off the handful of pursuers and get back to her home.

That night, in the company of an old and kindly Arab woman who had known her mother, she left Baikas. Fort Iama, she had heard, was not very far away. Only a few miles over the border. There she would seek safety.

They had to travel on foot — there were few horses or mules in Hanah.

But they made swift progress — until that night. Until midnight.

It was then that they passed through a large village which clustered near the old military road. And there they saw the mobs again.

They were gathering near the village. Streaming in from other communities, of which there were many in the area. And they brandished ancient swords, scimitars and muskets as they heard from their soldiers that a great Legion column was already moving into their land.

And again Lydia had to flee. If her white skin was seen, she would be slashed to pieces.

But first she persuaded the old Arab woman to stay. It was better for them to separate, for the venerable one was in no danger provided she was not seen in the company of Lydia.

That delay was almost fatal. The mob saw her as she moved out of the village. They called her back. Panic seized her, and she ran, thinking they would forget her once she was out of sight. But soon she knew that the mob was following her. Not deliberately, perhaps, but because they were taking the road which they knew the Legion would almost surely fellow.

Several times, when she rested exhausted, she saw their torches. Heard their wild chanting. And, like a flogged animal, she was compelled to run again.

To keep on running.

There was no safety in turning off the desert road. For she could not take a bearing from a star. She would lose herself and die if she did that.

It was thus that she ran into the column's advance patrol. Ran into the arms of those she was praying to see. But she had no time to taste even a temporary relief. For when she saw the feeble force of less than two score men, she knew that they would be massacred if they did not turn and retreat. And she had heard that the Legion never retreated.

★ ★ ★

Laubert was not impressed. He indicated the fact by an ungainly toss of his head. He even permitted himself a slight smile at Sergeant Horfal. But Horfal affected not to notice.

'You have wasted my time, and already it has been wasted enough. You do not imagine that a handful of rabble would interfere with us!'

She regarded him levelly.

'They are not a handful, *officier*. They are a multitude.'

'Could a multitude assemble in so short a time from the villages? You are afraid, woman, and in your fear you see ten men for every one that exists.'

She flushed. Brian noticed that the sudden flow of colour made her even lovelier.

But she said with flat composure: 'I wish I could see ten legionnaires for every one that exists.'

'Don't argue with me! We are continuing to Baikas — immediately. If you wish, you can proceed to Fort Iama until the country is pacified.'

'Alone, *officier?*'

'*Tiens!* Do you think I can spare an escort for you?'

'Then . . . how far is Fort Iama?'

'Nearly fifty kilometres.'

'I could never reach it. Not now — I am too weary. I might as well stay with you. And die with you!'

She uttered the pronouncement coldly, as though it was beyond contradiction. For the first time the legionnaires took their eyes off her. They glanced restively at each other.

Laubert swore. It was an obscene oath. Then he shouted: 'You are not a French national, and you are no concern of mine. I cannot be cluttered with an Arab waif!'

She stood up. Suddenly, her eyes were iced fury. She pulled back her rich lips so that the tips of her teeth showed.

'You forget, *officier*, my skin is white. I have white blood. And I am a woman. Does that mean nothing to you?'

For a moment Laubert seemed unsettled. But only for a moment. He drawled with heavy emphasis: 'The fact that you're a woman would have meant quite a lot to me — at any other time than this. But I am too busy, and too tired, to accept your favours now, *madam!*'

It was a cruel, deplorable insult.

It caused an indefinite shuffle among the legionnaires. Most of them were no better than they should be. Many were a lot worse than that. But, like most soldiers of most armies, they had beneath their outward crudities an innate sense of fairness.

She was standing less than a yard from Laubert.

From that position she sprang at him.

But it was not a wild, uncontrolled spring. It had something in common with the smooth, compact bound of a cat upon its prey.

Her sandaled feet were clear of the ground as she thudded softly against his chest. Laubert, who was taken completely by surprise, tried to pull her away. But he was too late. Too late. Too late to save his eyes from the short but sharp nails which dragged across them. They dug under the lids, ripped at each sensitive iris.

Brian was the first to reach her. By now, her slim arms had transferred to Laubert's neck, leaving great red furrows there. Viciously, he pulled her away. He pushed her back. Then Katz held her.

And Laubert was reeling in an uncertain circle, a hand across his face.

Horfal moved up to him.

'Let me look, *capitaine*,' he said.

Laubert let his hand drop to his side. Horfal let out a low hiss at what he saw. But he did not speak

He watched as Laubert took more vague, wobbling steps. All of them watched. And it was Laubert himself who spoke. His voice was no longer strong. No longer brutal. It was a whimper, like that of a child who does not understand.

'I cannot see!' he said. 'I'm blind . . . '

He pushed his hands in front of him, as if hoping to feel his way. No one moved towards him. No one took his arm. They gazed upon him like dream figures watching a nightmare.

'*Where am I . . . ? I cannot see . . . *'

141

He raised his head as though in supplication to the heavens. At the same time he staggered round so that he faced the column. A mutter went up when they saw in fading moonlight what had become of his sight.

Then someone laughed. A harsh, merciless laugh that came from the rear of the column. And a voice bawled out of the shadows: 'Give him his gun, Sergeant Horfal! Maybe he wants to play Russian roulette!!'

Horfal looked in the direction of the voice, tried to identify it, but could not. Without speaking, he turned again to Laubert. Now he extended a hand and held the captain's elbow.

'I will put a dressing on it, *mon capitaine.*'

That same raucous voice came again from the column.

'Why not put a bullet in him, instead, sergeant?'

This time, several others gave support. Their wild shouts pierced the night air. Their demands were expressed in an assortment of tongues, but they amounted to the same thing.

'He's asked for it!'

'It's his own medicine . . . '

'We can't carry a blind pig around . . . '

'Put him out of his misery . . . '

Brian listened. Those men who were shouting for retribution against a helpless man — they were not really like that. Brian knew it. Under ordinary circumstances they could be as merciful as most. But these were not ordinary circumstances. This was the harvest that Laubert himself had sown.

Laubert had created an atmosphere of perverted evil. He was being treated with evil.

A legionnaire said something in an undertone. It made those near him laugh. Then, apparently repeating the words, he bawled: 'Let Katz shoot him! Katz would enjoy that!'

The little Austrian had been standing close to Brian. And Brian heard him swear — which was unusual.

Katz slung his Lebel. In a few short, quick steps he reached the column. He asked quietly: 'Who said that?'

A brief, strained silence followed the

question. Then a burly, bald-headed Dane said: 'It was me, Katz.'

'You did, uh! Would you kill a man who can no longer see?'

The Dane smiled. He was inches taller than Katz and looked heavily down on him.

'So you are afraid of him. Even now you are afraid Well, you may snivel to Laubert, but not . . . '

The Dane did not know Katz well. If he had, he might have taken warning from the Austrian's slight change in stance. His right foot eased back. He switched most of his weight to the left. Then he swung his right fist.

It was not an orthodox punch. It was certainly not a correct punch, for through leading with that fist he was wide open to a counter. But it had the cardinal advantage of being completely unexpected. And Katz, although small, carried plenty of muscle power.

His knuckles slapped against the angle of the Dane's jaw. There was a sharp, hollow sound. The man's head went back, as though on a hinge.

He would have fallen had he not staggered against the others. As it was, his knees dipped and his eyes were momentarily glazed. It was not a knock-out punch that Katz had delivered. But it was a very damaging one.

And Katz did not wait to study the effect. He moved in to hit again.

The quiet, good-natured, thoughtful, easy-going Katz . . .

It was typical of him that when he did a thing he did it very thoroughly. As a student in Vienna, his work had been thorough. It was the same when he organised resistance against the Nazis in his beloved city. And when, through calamitous ill-fortune he had been compelled to become a soldier, he had become a thoroughly efficient and courageous one.

And when he lost his temper — which was very rare — there were no half-measures about it.

He aimed another vicious punch at the Dane. But it missed because the column had now lost all semblance of formation and several men knocked into him.

A man with a heavy Italian accent

145

shouted: 'Let them fight it out! Let them fight for Laubert! If Katz wins, Laubert can live!'

Brian and Horfal pushed through the mob towards Katz.

And Brian thought: 'It's happening again . . . the whole discipline's falling apart . . .'

Horfal reached Katz first. He put a hand on the Austrian's arm and pulled him firmly away from the crush. There was silence. Horfal used it to speak. He did so fiercely.

'You're no longer soldiers! You scum! You yattering rabble! Have you forgotten something? Have you forgotten that a few miles from here there are helpless civilians in danger of being butchered? But perhaps *they* are not worrying too much! Perhaps they are thinking all will be well, for the Legion is on the way! *The Legion!* That's you! You, *mes braves!* Look at you! You spit on the corpses of the men who died to make this army great . . .'

He paused. All those round him had become very still. Horfal was sweating. He raised an impassioned hand as he continued: 'Do you hate *mon capitaine* any more now than you did five minutes ago? You do not. Then why did I not hear talk of killing him when he had eyes to see? I will tell you ... You knew you needed his brain, his experience to get us through this operation alive. For the sake of your own miserable skins you were willing to let him live! But now he can no longer lead you, now he is of no more use to you, you howl for his life ... That is the talk of cowards. It is not worthy of men!'

Long before he had finished, Horfal had won. He had restored balance. He had done so by preaching the doctrine of shame. He was a wise veteran, was Sergeant Horfal.

And, anticipating an inevitable question, he added in a suddenly softened tone: 'Captain Laubert's days as a soldier are over for a very long time. Perhaps for good. But our task now is to reach the legation — and take him with us. We will do that. Nothing — nothing between hell and heaven must stop us!'

A black American said in a slow drawl:

'He'll need someone to lead him.'

Horfal nodded, reminded of a difficulty. For Laubert was now as helpless as a babe. He could see absolutely nothing. And, because his blindness was new, he would have no confidence in any man who attempted to act as a guide. He would walk slowly, reluctantly.

Yes — he would walk very slowly.

He would slow the column to a snail's pace. And the orders were to reach Baikas quickly . . .

'He'll have to be carried,' Horfal said. 'We'll have to make a litter of some sort. Two knotted blankets will serve . . . '

Laubert shouted.

It was a petulant, confused shout. The call of a man who is mystified. It came from some way off.

They swung round.

At first they could not detect him.

Then, a mere fifty yards ahead, they saw the Arabs. They were standing still and massed deep across the road and beyond it on either side. Some of them flickered faintly, for dawn was at hand.

Laubert was among them. He was

struggling feebly, while two of them held him.

Each man in the column knew what had happened.

Laubert, the unseeing Laubert, had wandered into the ranks of the Arabs while his men had been scuffling and arguing.

8

Total Loss

'Par nombres . . . ouvert!'

Horfal gave the order automatically — a pure reflex from a numbed brain. It was obeyed in the same fashion. Moving in sequence of their column numbers, the legionnaires spread out in a single thin line.

'Fusil!'

There was a harsh, mechanical rattling as thirty-five hands cocked the firing pins of thirty-five rifles.

'Garde!'

The Lebel butts were dug under the armpits, the barrels slightly inclined towards the ground. From this stance a firing position could be assumed in a moment. And it did not impose the physical strain involved in holding a heavy rifle against the shoulder for any prolonged period.

Brian and Katz — because they had

been detached to advance patrol — had lost their column number. But they had inserted themselves in the centre of the flank, immediately behind where Horfal stood. Brian noticed the girl. Or it would be more correct to state that he sensed the girl. Lydia was standing almost directly behind him. He heard her fast, light breathing. He heard her give a little moan.

Horfal walked ten paces towards the Arabs. The Spaniard's rifle was slung from his shoulder, was swinging like a toy as he came to a crisp halt. He shouted in Arabic: 'Leave the officer alone! If you harm him, we fire!'

The Arab mob had been silent. But now they broke into a raucous babble. Two of them continued to hold Laubert, but beyond restraining his feeble resistance they were not harming him.

Horfal directed a swift, analytical glance at the Arab ranks. Two facts were obvious. First — the mob was badly armed. A few possessed muskets. There were one or two soldiers among them (presumably from the force which the

151

column had already routed) and these had rifles. But the rest were equipped only with swords and knives. Second — Laubert had been right when he had accused the girl of exaggerating their numbers because of fear. They totalled no more than a couple of hundred.

Horfal saw that this rabble could offer no serious menace as a fighting force. They could be decimated by a couple of volleys.

But they held Laubert.

And while they continued to hold Laubert it would be impossible to fire on them without killing him.

The Spaniard recalled another point, too.

The column was under orders to avoid conflict, if it was possible. They were entitled to use force only if it was necessary to reach and protect the civilians in the Baikas legation.

At first it seemed that the Arabs were entirely without leadership, for they all talked at the same time. Some directed incomprehensible remarks to Horfal. Others shouted at each other. But suddenly the row subsided. A young, well-built man in a tattered burnous had pushed his way to the front and held up his arms for silence. The fact that he was obeyed indicated that he had some special status.

With studied precision, the Arab advanced in the same way that Horfal had done, taking the same number of paces, so that a mere thirty yards separated the two men. As soon as he spoke it was apparent that the Arab was a fanatic. A man without any special intelligence, but impelled by a mass of wrong opinions based on an array of misconceptions. In that respect he had much in common with all fanatics of all races.

He said: 'You have come to ravage and despoil our land and we will have vengeance . . .'

Ostensibly, this was directed at Horfal. But in fact it was obviously for the consumption of the rabble behind him. And it had its effect. There was a rumble of support and fury which ended when he again raised a hand. Horfal let him continue.

'It seems your officer has already tasted

the vengeance of my people. And now he belongs to us. We will hold him . . . unless you turn and face the way you have come. We will let him go free when every legionnaire has left our soil. That is our pledge,'

Beyond the impossibility of the suggestion, Horfal knew that the pledge was almost certainly worthless. Left in their hands, the already suffering Laubert would be put to death with exquisite and unholy deliberation.

Horfal rubbed the scars on his lean face. They became patches of pink amid the copper skin. He said: 'Do you understand the French tongue?'

The Arab was surprised. He inclined his head in assent.

'Then I will count in French. I will count to five. If the officer is not free by then, I will give the order to fire.'

'I am not deceived. You would not kill your officer.'

'We will not shoot at him.'

'But you would slay him, just the same. A volley aimed at my people would also strike the Frenchman, see . . . how could it be otherwise? He is held in the front, and the others are gathered behind.'

That was true. The mob had clustered into a congealed mass directly to the rear of those who were holding Laubert.

Horfal said, in a matter-of-fact tone: 'We will not aim at your people. We will aim at you. At you alone. Every rifle will be directed at you . . . no! Don't move! Stay where you are, my talkative friend. Listen to me while I count. And remember, you have but five moments to release the captain.

'*Une . . . deux . . . trois . . .* '

The Arab was no hero. His voice was pitched at a quavering scream as he turned and gave the order to free Laubert.

It was obeyed without hesitation. Probably not because the rabble had any particular affection for their leader, but because Horfal had gained an absolute moral ascendancy. They possessed only the courage of hysteria. Horfal's iced exactness frightened them.

Laubert, freed from support, staggered pathetically forward a few paces, hands stretched before him. Then he lost balance and fell. He tried to get up. But in his blindness he tripped over his own feet and sprawled again.

Horfal said to the young Arab: 'Help him up — and do it carefully. Then bring him here.'

The man looked at the line of legionnaires. Looked at the taut, formidable Horfal. Then he bent over Laubert. With some difficulty he pulled the weighty captain to his feet. He guided him to Horfal.

The sergeant gave a curt nod of approval.

It was much more than a pure utilitarian order that he had given to the deflated fanatic. By making him assist Laubert he had, completed the man's humiliation. And, indirectly, he had abased the mob. Now they were no longer threatening and dangerous. They were timid and docile.

The young Arab stopped a yard from Horfal. He still held Laubert.

Horfal said to him: 'You are going to help me. We are going to know each other well. What's your name?'

'I am Vyaam, of the village of . . . '

'Never mind that. It was only your

name that I asked for. Very well, Vyaam. Now answer this question — and answer it truthfully. Are any more of your people gathering on this road?'

'There are no others. Our soldiers brought the tale of your invasion but a short time ago, and we gathered to repel you. But the story had not spread further.'

Horfal permitted himself one of his quick smiles. There was little doubt that Vyaam was speaking the truth. He was not in a condition to do otherwise. And his statement meant that there would be no more delays from the Arabs at least until they got within sight of Baikas . . . unless this mob in front of him streamed ahead and gave warning of the column's approach. And Horfal had no intention of allowing this to happen. He intended not only to render the Arabs harmless, but to make them useful, too.

He said: 'Listen to me carefully, Vyaam. I have decided that you and your men will lead us into Baikas.'

'Lead you! But we cannot . . . '

'You can and you will. All of you will walk a little way ahead of the column.

Not too far. If any man attempts to break away he will be shot in the back. There will be no warning.'

Vyaam was confused, scared and baffled. Each emotion showed clearly on his immature face.

He bleated: 'But why? This, the road the French made, goes straight into Baikas. None can get lost.'

'We are not worried about getting lost. I want to be sure you do not give advance warning of our approach. But that is not all, my friend. You are going to tell any other Arabs we may meet on the way that we come in peace. You understand?'

Horfal's words, spoken in slow, clear Arabic, reached all the subdued rabble. He allowed time for the full meaning to become clear.

Then he added: 'But three of your men and your self will march with us. You will make a litter and carry the captain upon it.'

Vyaam showed a flicker — it was no more than a flicker — of indignation.

'I am not a beast of burden. I am a leader. I will choose four . . . '

'You will choose three of your men, Vyaam. You will be the fourth. You will make the litter as you wish out of your robes, and each of you will carry a corner of it.'

That ended the argument.

Under Horfal's direction, some of the Arabs tore sections off their clothing. These were knotted and plaited to form a single strong sheet large enough to hold a man.

When it was ready, Horfal turned to Laubert. It was now almost full daylight, and the early sun was shining full on the captain's ghastly, sightless eyes. He was standing very still, afraid to move through his personal darkness. And now he was absolutely quiet. Not even a moan of pain from him.

Horfal said with formal respect: 'Did you hear my orders, *mon capitaine?*'

Laubert's answer was little more than a whisper.

'*Oui*. You are doing well, sergeant. But . . . let us get to Baikas quickly. There . . . there must be a doctor in the legation . . . '

159

Horfal regarded him thoughtfully. He noticed what they all had noticed — that Laubert's first thought was no longer for the civilians.

Katz eased forward. He was holding a small package of bandage which each legionnaire carried in his *capote*. Katz said diffidently: 'Shall I . . . ?'

'Yes, put it on the captain. It won't do much good — except to keep the flies away.'

Katz unwound the material. He said to Laubert: '*Mon capitaine, I* am going to bandage your eyes. You will feel more comfortable.'

Laubert did not answer. Katz wound the material round his head. But it slipped. He pulled it off as gently as he could, but Laubert grunted with pain.

He was about to start again when Lydia moved up to him. They had forgotten about Lydia. She looked dazed, tense. She held out a hand for the bandage. And she said softly: 'I will do it. I know how.'

Before Katz had fully realised what had happened, she had taken the material from him. Then she turned to Laubert.

He backed away, almost falling again. 'If it's that she-cat, take her away . . . *take her away!*'

He screamed the final few words. His contused face pulsated, showing supreme terror.

Lydia did not attempt to follow him. She said: 'I can't atone for what I have done — but will you not let me try to help you?'

The words were utterly humble. Utterly sincere.

Laubert became calmer. He ceased to back away. He said viciously: 'I'll have you rotting in a prison for this! You have taken away my sight! You'll suffer, you raceless she-cat!'

'I hope I do suffer. I would not complain if every bone in my wretched body is broken because of the evil I have done to you . . . now let me cover your eyes.'

Although Laubert was not a tall man, she had to stand on her toes to wrap the material round his head. And now Laubert accepted the attention. All the fury was drained out of him.

Watching intently, Brian noticed that she had fine, nimble hands. They worked deftly with the roll of bandage. When she had finished, Laubert was no longer repulsive to look upon.

And it was she who guided Laubert to the litter. She who arranged him on it after taking off his tunic and folding it as a pillow.

Brian was still watching her when he fell in with the column.

He could not understand why, but he knew a surge of raw fury as he saw that she was walking at the side of the litter. And it was obvious that she had no thought for anyone or anything — save the man she had blinded.

★   ★   ★

Baikas was almost entirely a French creation.

True, since the first quivering start of human time there had been Arab habitations there. But the French, during their occupation, had seen the commercial and military possibilities of the place

162

and developed them.

Commercially, Baikas relied on its nearby silver mines. These were moderately rich, and the metal was brought into the capital for extraction and refining.

The mines were developed under the auspices of the French government. And when the state of Hanah was granted independence, they remained French property under the treaty terms. Thus a handful of white mining engineers, metallurgists and chemists remained in the capital.

From the military point of view, Baikas had been important to the French because a base there enabled forces to be moved rapidly to any point in the entire Hanah territory, and to other southern areas beyond. The withdrawal of French forces from the country had caused considerable misgivings among the High Command and General Staff, because it meant that the only remaining base in an area of some twenty thousand square miles was Fort Iama.

So the French made Baikas. They made it a place with a small European business centre of broad boulevards. A place with a scattering of modern government buildings which the new Arab government took over when the French moved out. And they unwittingly created a city of squalor and poverty in the big native quarter. For Arabs — attracted by exaggerated tales of the wealth to be gained there — had settled in huge numbers in Baikas. Far greater numbers than the city was able to support. The result for many was a perpetual state of near starvation.

But, bad though the lot of the native population had been during the French occupation, it became vastly worse after they left. For all who possessed even the most meagre possessions were taxed ruthlessly to support a corrupt government of their own people.

That, as the column had already heard, had been the reason for the revolt among part of the Hanah army. A revolt which had leapt out of control and was now in the hands of maddened mobs.

And that was the city which the column — headed by an advance guard of two hundred frightened and reluctant Arabs — approached in the mid-afternoon.

On the whole, the advance to Baikas had gone well under Sergeant Horfal's command. Possibly too well.

There had been difficulties, but they had not been great ones. All of them came from the Arabs at the front.

Vyaam's motley rabble fully understood what was expected of them. They knew that they had to move in a compact body a few yards beyond the front of the column. And that, if called upon to do so, they were to shout expressions of reassurance and joy at the entry of the Legion into their territory.

This they did on several occasions, for as they got nearer Baikas the land became more fertile and the villages more frequent. And in those places the populations, at first hostile at the sight of French uniforms, were nonplussed when they saw that their countrymen were apparently leading them and approving of them. For Vyaam's men, convinced that they would be shot in the back if they did not obey, called words of eager support for the Legion.

It was in the matter of speed that the Arabs proved difficult.

Several times Horfal had to halt his column because it threatened to merge with the faltering Arabs. In response to threats, they would quicken their pace for a short time, then revert to their normal ambling pace.

The result had been delay — infuriating delay.

But now the march was almost over. And there was an unreal aspect about their approach to the outskirts of the city. On each side was scrubland and patches of sand — seeming even more barren and hopeless than the virgin desert. But there were also hints of western civilisation. A wooden villa, for example, its windows smashed and doors kicked in where the mobs had looted. It stood in the neglected remnants of a garden. Obviously, a French family had once had their home there. Probably the family was now in the legation — if the legation was still there. On the side of the road they saw a wrecked Renault motor car. In all probability it had been seized by some of the mob and driven wildly out of Baikas, then abandoned after a crash.

And — most weird of all to men who had not seen such things for many months — there was the traffic sign. It stood on a bent steel pole and was grimed with sand. But it was a relic of the French administration. And it gave Horfal precisely the information he required.

It announced: *Baikas 3 kilometres.*

They were almost there. It was only because they were at the foot of a slight incline that the city was not visible in the distance.

Horfal shouted a command. The column halted. The Arabs halted, too. Gratefully.

For a few seconds Horfal regarded the men strung along the road. He swore to himself, and dabbed his sweating face with his sleeve. Then he turned to Vyaam, who was still holding his corner of the litter in which Laubert dozed uneasily.

'Put it down,' he said. 'And come here.'

Vyaam trotted towards him, rubbing a weary arm. His spirit was entirely broken. He feared Horfal as he had never feared any man.

Horfal asked: 'To which side of the city

does this road take us?'

'To the western side, *effendi*.'

'I know that, you miserable fool! Does it lead into the Arab quarter?'

Vyaam shook his head eagerly.

'No. You enter our city through the places where the French and our despicable government ministers lived.'

'And then?'

'Then you are in the middle of Baikas.'

'Where is the French legation?'

'In the middle of Baikas. You will not miss it, *effendi*. There are great crowds round it, I am told.'

Horfal hesitated. He looked towards the Arabs, who were squatting exhausted on the ground. It was clear to him that they were no longer useful. Frightened though they were, it would be impossible to control them once they entered crowded streets. In fact, if they were allowed in Baikas, Vyaam and his men would probably recover their nerve and inflame the city mobs against the legionnaires.

He had to get rid of them.

Horfal stretched out a lean but muscular hand. It gripped Vyaam's tattered burnous. It twisted the material so that the man's clothing became tight around his body.

'Listen to me carefully, Vyaam — are you listening?'

'Yes.'

'That is good. Do you know what you and your rabble are going to do now?'

'We are going to guide you into the city.'

'You are not. You are going to turn back and return to the hovels you came from.'

At first Vyaam appeared relieved. Then a faint suggestion of duplicity spread over his face. Horfal saw it. He tightened his grip.

'And if you attempt to enter the city and warn the people, you will die before you get near it! We will be waiting for you! Now tell your men to get to their feet — and run! If you are not all out of sight in five minutes we will open fire on you. Start! And thank Allah for my great mercy!'

The rabble did not need any further instructions from Vyaam. They streamed westward past the column. Exhausted though they were, most of them attained a surprising speed.

As they watched them disappear, Brian said to Horfal:

'Do you think any of them'll try to slip back?'

Horfal shook his head.

'No. Not once they are out of sight. Weary men do not willingly do the same journey three times. The spirit has gone out of them. But they never had much spirit in them. They are stupid, cowardly men from the villages. I only hope we find the city mobs of Baikas as easy to manage.'

He spoke without much optimism.

But Brian was scarcely listening. He had noticed Lydia. Despite her exhaustion, she looked as lovely as ever. Like a child. Very small, very slender. Her face, sullied by sand, still showed oddly white. So did her long hair.

She was kneeling beside Laubert. She was holding a pad of cloth which she had dampened from the captain's water-bottle. And with it she was wiping his greasy brow.

Laubert, who had suddenly awakened,

was talking to her. Brian was too far away to pick up the whispered words. Nor could he hear her reply. But she smiled as she spoke. An infinitely soft, understanding smile. It was almost impossible to believe that it came from a woman who had caused the ghastly injuries. It was a smile which reflected the other woman within this pure white half-caste. The normal woman — gentle, kind.

9

Into Baikas

To move into the city immediately — or wait until darkness?

That was the problem with which Horfal wrestled. And it was not as simple as it first appeared.

There was much to be said for waiting. During the hours of darkness the city — even a city torn by civil war — would be much quieter than during the day. Presumably the mob formed a permanent ring round the legation. But it would not be so strong or so difficult to penetrate with the night as an ally.

Horfal reminded himself that he had to get Laubert through on the litter. Now that the Arabs were gone, four legionnaires would have to be detached to carry him. And the girl would have to be protected. Both would be a particularly attractive bait for a mob in the daylight, whereas they might not be noticed at night.

But . . .

His orders were to reach the legation as soon as possible. It was now twenty-six hours since the signal from the High Command had reached Fort Iama. Despite forced marches, they were two hours and more behind schedule. And for all that he, Horfal, knew, the position in the legation might have become even more critical. Perhaps, even at this moment, the mobs were breaking through the cordons of Hanah soldiers and conducting a massacre in the building . . .

What was he to do? March now? Or wait?

Horfal walked a few restless paces up and down the road while the column watched him curiously.

He had a quick, agile brain, had Horfal. He would never have attained his rank if he had not, for the required standard of education and training for Legion N.C.O.s was higher than that of any other army on earth — including the British and American. But this was not a tactical problem, such as might normally fall within the province of a senior sergeant. It was a question involving factors on the strategic level, with which he had never been trained to deal. A question which Laubert would have analysed and decided upon without hesitation, for Laubert had the training. Laubert would have seen which course was the right one, Horfal told himself.

Horfal stopped abruptly during his pacing. Laubert was blind. But his brain was still there. Why not ask him? Why not outline the situation and ask for his decision?

Yes — he would do that.

Horfal moved towards the litter, which lay on the softer scrub just off the road. He noticed that the girl was kneeling beside it and holding Laubert's wrist.

'I wish to speak to *le capitaine*. You will leave us for a few minutes.'

'He is sleeping again. You must not wake him.'

'I'm sorry — but I'll have to wake him. It's important. I need a decision from him — now.'

He was surprised at her reaction. Gently, she put his hand across his chest.

Then she stood up. Her large blue eyes glittered.

'Is it that you want to ask him what to do?'

There was a heavy load of contempt in her queerly enunciated French. Horfal was annoyed at the accuracy of her guess.

'Do not ask questions. I will wake him . . . '

'You will leave him alone!'

Horfal had an uneasy feeling that he had seen her like this before. Then he remembered. She had pulsated with the same sudden savagery before she had attacked Laubert. Now her fury was in defence of Laubert . . .

Horfal decided to reason with her.

'You must understand — this is very necessary. It's vital. I must have his opinion on a . . . '

'Are you so feeble yourself that you have to lean upon him? Look at him, sergeant! He is blind and he is ill! And I made him like that! But I will not add to my crime by allowing you to torture him with your questions. Keep away from him! If you want to help him, do so by getting to the legation as soon as you can, instead of talking here. He says there will be a doctor at the legation.'

She stood, arms akimbo, glaring at him. A miniature epitome of defiance. And Horfal suddenly knew that she had given him the answer. Laubert himself tipped the scales. They could not leave him there for the rest of the day, under the ferocious sun. Better to face the risks, and move at once into Baikas.

$$\star \quad \star \quad \star$$

Horfal called Legionnaire Brian Sayle out of the column. He said to him: 'You were an officer in the British Army, huh?'

'Yes. I was attached to the Third Commando.'

'I have heard. I have seen your enlistment papers. Your Commandos had much experience of street fighting . . . of operations in towns and confined areas?'

'Yes, we had.'

'I have had no such experience since the Spanish civil war, and then it was not much. Mostly we fought in the open. And since I have been in the Legion all my work has been in the desert lands. That is why I need your advice.'

Brian failed to conceal his surprise. In his experience, N.C.O.s were not inclined to ask for the views of rankers. Horfal noticed his expression.

'The Legion is an unusual army,' he said. 'We have men in it with many qualifications such as you would not find in any other military force. We N.C.O.s would be very stupid if we did not make good use of that fact. That is why I am going to ask you what a British Commando unit would do if they had to reach a building in a hostile town while protecting a helpless man and a woman. I want you to think that you are an officer again. How would you deploy these men?'

Brian forced himself to think in terms of British tactical deployment. He recalled the brief, bloody and successful raid on St. Nazaire in 1942. That had been a classic . . . They had fought their way out of the town while carrying scores of their wounded. And there had been not a trace of panic. No apparent hurry. Everything had moved according to a timed schedule.

But this would be different in many respects from St. Nazaire. The legionnaires were not accustomed to close combat. In any case, they had to avoid fighting, if they could. And their total strength was only thirty-five. A ridiculous number.

'I am waiting, legionnaire,' Horfal said.

'When we enter the city I would deploy in diamond formation.'

'Diamond formation? What is that?'

'Four equal lines of men.'

'But that is a square!'

'Not quite, *mon sergeant*. The men move forward with only one of the angles of the square at the front.'

'Ah! So it *looks* like a diamond, uh?'

'Yes. And the two foremost sides face forward and outward. The rear sides face backward and outward. In that way every angle is covered.'

Horfal was quick to see the simple ingenuity of this formation. He nodded enthusiastically.

'The four men carrying Laubert would be in the middle. The woman, too.'

'They would. And they'd have the best

possible protection.'

'Where does the commanding officer place himself?'

'In the centre.'

Horfal's eyebrows shot up.

'You don't mean to tell me that in the British Army the man in command skulks behind the backs of his troops?'

Brian was mildly indignant.

'Certainly not. But when you use diamond formation the centre is the only possible place for the, commander — it's only there that he can see everything that's happening. If he takes a position in any of the four sides he will only be able to see directly in front of him.'

Horfal looked doubtful.

'That may be so. But I am not going to place myself with a wounded man and a woman.'

'You must, *mon sergeant*, or you won't be able to take command. There will be no leadership. Someone has to have an overall picture.'

Horfal shrugged a pair of reluctant shoulders. 'Well . . . if I must, I will. It is all very strange to me. But to work . . . '

Strange or not, Horfal showed a swift ability to put the fighting tactic into operation.

After Brian had resumed his place in the column, Horfal selected four fresh men to take charge of the litter. Then he ordered the thirty others to form a single file. They numbered off. The numbers one to sixteen deployed into two sides of eight men each. Seventeen to thirty completed a slightly imperfect square — it was imperfect because the total strength was not exactly divisible by four. But this was of no real importance.

There followed some necessarily unmilitary shuffling while Horfal adjusted the square so that one corner of it made an apex, so giving the diamond shape.

Then the litter bearers and Lydia moved into the middle. They were followed by an embarrassed Horfal, who obviously had not reconciled himself to this station.

From the central position Horfal explained the purpose of the formation. The rear men adjusted their stance so that they faced half back. The front men turned half out.

The manoeuvre was accompanied by

some under-breath cursing, such as is the eternal prerogative of soldiers who are fumbling with the unfamiliar.

'That,' Horfal said, 'will be our formation through the streets of Baikas. But until we reach the crowds you will all face forwards. Keep the diamond shape, though, while we march . . . '

Brian, who was on the right front immediately behind Katz, smiled spontaneously as he heard Horfal add, after a diffident cough: 'I am in the middle because it is the only place where I can watch everything. Now remember — never lose formation. Listen for my orders. Listen hard, because you won't be able to see me. And do not do so much as stroke a trigger unless I say so . . . *Fix bayonets!*'

The order was unexpected. But the legionnaires' hands went automatically to the scabbards. There was a brief series of metallic clicks as the long blades slid on to the barrel clips.

As he fixed his own bayonet, Brian took a swift glance into the centre. A glance towards Lydia. She was kneeling again. Kneeling beside Laubert, whose litter had been placed on the ground. She was gently adjusting the bandage over his sightless eyes. Her own eyes were moist with tears.

★   ★   ★

They seemed to enter the outskirts of the city abruptly. They saw it as a sprawling mass from the top of the incline. It was lost to view as they descended. Then, suddenly, the road broadened and they were in a residential avenue. Bungalows were on either side. All of them cruelly wrecked by the vandals. In these homes the French and the prosperous Arabs had lived.

Here there were few people about. Just a scattered handful of mendicant Arabs lazing in the despoiled gardens or sprawling hopelessly on the sidewalks.

Katz said over his shoulder to Brian: 'Baikas seems a quiet place!'

Brian did not answer. He had a feeling that this condition was not to last for long.

He was right.

At first the few Arabs stared unbelievingly at the legionnaires. They chattered excitedly to each other. Then some of them ran ahead shouting hysterical warnings. Others kept pace with the column, but at a respectful distance from the bayonets.

Arabs are the world's most expert people at forming themselves into a mob. They can do so at a speed which is miraculous. The Arabs of Baikas were no exception.

Within minutes — and as if from nowhere — the sides of the avenue were thronged with hundreds of bellowing, gesticulating men, women and children. And more were joining them each moment.

But they were not yet impeding the column's progress. They kept to the sides of the road.

Horfal shouted: 'At the double — march!'

They quickened their pace to a trot.

From one point of view it was a good order, because it enabled them to cover a lot of ground while the path ahead was clear. But on the other hand, the spectacle of legionnaires breaking into a run injected extra confidence into the mob. It suggested — quite wrongly — a state of panic.

The Arabs — who now numbered at least a thousand — ran too. And suddenly they flooded over the road in front. They spread out behind. They came closer on either side. The detachment was encircled.

Horfal immediately countermanded his order. They resumed a regulation marching pace.

Then he called: 'Forward lines face out . . . rear lines face back . . . take marching time from me . . . '

He called a very slow time now, necessary because half of the men were progressing backwards, in a crab-wise fashion.

Above the din of the mob Brian heard oaths from the men at the rear. He understood why. They held by far the most awkward position. And the whole column was attempting to put into action a formation which, in the ordinary way, called for much parade-ground practice. And this was no parade-ground. Brian wondered whether he had been wise to make the suggestion.

But he need not have worried on that score.

After the first few moments, the legionnaires settled down to their unnatural mode of progress.

As he walked, Horfal turned slowly, surveying the whole scene. Over the heads of his men he could see nothing but a fluttering, congealed, vicious conglomeration of humanity. In front, they parted reluctantly to let them through. At all other points they were close — too close. The perpetual yelling from the many hundreds of throats made the ears ring. The sickly smell from the unclean bodies revolted the nostrils.

But, on the whole, Horfal was satisfied. So long as they were able to make progress without having to use force, they had nothing to worry about.

He spared a moment to look at the litter and at Lydia. The woman was obviously very afraid. But she had courage, he told himself. There was a defiant tilt to her chin. And she was holding Laubert's hand again. Laubert . . . he might still be asleep. He lay completely inert.

Horfal's evanescent conjecture about Lydia and Laubert ended abruptly. It ended when he felt a cruel stabbing pain at the top of his right shoulder. Other nerves reacted, and the back of his neck tingled unpleasantly. He was momentarily confused. Then something clattered to the ground between his legs. It was a jagged piece of rock. It must have been thrown with a high trajectory. Only his webbing shoulder strap had saved him from serious injury.

The Arabs were using the eternal weapon of a rabble.

There was a brief interval of comparative quiet after the first stone had been thrown. A lull during which the others absorbed the idea and searched for some thing to throw. There was no shortage of this sort of ammunition. It was strewn all over the road.

Presently the air seemed to be filled with missiles. And not all of them were stones. Pieces of wood and even razor-sharp fragments of glass from the ruined houses were directed at the detachment.

The aim, naturally, was bad. The Arabs, being congested, seldom had sufficient space to swing their arms properly. The result was that many of the projectiles passed over their target. Others fell short, injuring other Arabs.

But a few found their mark.

A square of heavy teak wood hit Katz on the chin. It was a glancing blow, but he grunted with pain. Blood dribbled from a graze of the skin. But the Austrian did not falter in his slow stride.

Another legionnaire was struck on a knee. He swore and hobbled for a few moments. And the big Dane stopped an exceptionally large stone in the chest. It drove him sideways into the centre of the formation, where he crashed into Horfal.

Horfal steadied him. Then pointed to the open space which the man had left.

'Get back!'

The Dane was breathing with difficulty. He had been badly winded.

'Give me a minute, sergeant — I'm hurt.'

'Get back now! You know the danger.'

The Dane made an acrid comment. But he realised the threat presented by a wide gap in the diamond formation. He stumbled back into his place.

Now Horfal knew a new torment.

The formation was wavering.

Instinctively, the legionnaires were

watching for the missiles and trying to duck away from them. Bayonets no longer pointed solidly outwards in a menacing barrier of steel. They wavered and dipped as their owners sought to avoid the barrage.

Horfal drew in a heavy breath, then shouted: 'Keep still — if you lose station they'll rush you!'

Perhaps his words were unheard amid the clamour of the mob. Or perhaps the legionnaires did not choose to heed them. In any case, there was no reaction to the order. The formation quickly assumed a ragged, uneven and indefinite shape.

And Horfal knew the legionnaires could not be blamed. No experience is more unnerving than that of being stoned.

He was debating whether to take extreme action when the man they called Happy was killed.

Happy (of course) was a perpetually mournful specimen. He was a Bulgarian, and he seemed to resent the fact. He was one of those men who resent every thing. He glared at the world through a black cloud of miserable hostility. He appeared to enjoy sorrow. Yet this long-faced legionnaire was fundamentally good-natured. He would lend his last fifty francs while reading a lecture on the evils of borrowing. He would cover up for a man who was absent at *appel*, then declaim to high heaven against comrades who shirked their duty. Almost everyone liked Happy. He was the perfect foil for crude wit. His morose demeanour could add joy to any off-duty celebration. The best testimonial for a bawdy story was the untrue statement that it was enough to make Happy laugh.

A lump of rock hit Happy on the forehead.

It had been thrown from only a few yards away. The velocity was vicious. It ripped open the thin flesh, revealing white bone.

For a couple of seconds after he was struck, Happy the Bulgarian trudged on in his position at the front of the formation. But his eyes were glazed, his mouth slack.

Then suddenly his brain went numb.

His rifle dropped. The bayonet caught between his legs. He stumbled over it. He swayed like a sapling giving to a storm.

And before he could be caught he had reeled into the clutching arms of the mob.

For moments they held him like spiders who have seen a fly drop into a web. Then they closed round him.

Horfal bawled for the column to halt. The order was superfluous. They had already done so. All were staring horrified at the place where Happy had been.

For, at the moment, he was no longer visible. The only clue to his presence was a localised whirlpool of activity. A scuffling of brown bodies. An agitation of tattered robes.

The stimulus of agony restored the Bulgarian to full consciousness.

The agony of hands.

Hands digging at his face. Hands tearing at his throat. Savage, pitiless, inhuman hands.

He shrieked. The sound quavered through and over the mob. It seemed to hold still in the air, an indictment against the barbarities of man.

The legionnaires gazed, still and silent.

Until, for a brief second, they saw the Bulgarian.

And then he disappeared.

Among the legionnaires, the spectacle broke the spell of immobility.

Several of them turned inwards towards Horfal. They started to shout together at the sergeant.

'We're going in to get him . . . '

'We've got to pull him out . . . '

'Are you going to leave him there . . . ?'

Horfal's head had started to ache fiercely. He battled against instinct. It was his instinct which urged him to agree with the legionnaires. To give an order which would cut the column loose, drive in among the mob and drag the Bulgarian out of it.

But logic warned him that that would be a calamitous thing to do. At bayonet point they would reach the man. There could be no doubt of that. He might even still be living when they did so. But the success would be ridiculously temporary, utterly futile. Within a few more moments they would be divided and each suffer the same fate as the man they hoped to save.

This, Horfal realised, was an opportunity to gain ground. But to seize that opportunity he must be ruthless.

There was icy fury in his tones as he shouted back: 'Get into formation! If we go in there, we won't last two minutes . . . can't you see? This is our chance . . . at the double!'

The diamond shape re-formed, for even the dullest of the men saw now what he meant. In these moments most of the mob had forgotten about the detachment. They were busy murdering the Bulgarian. Or trying to get close enough to assist in the murder. Miraculously, the stones had ceased to fly. And the ring round them was no longer unbroken. There was a clear space ahead.

As the entire detachment faced forward and broke again into a trot, Horfal took another look at Laubert and those around him.

The captain was sitting half-upright in his litter. The girl, while running, was trying to persuade him to lie flat. None of them was hurt.

Now their advance into the centre of Baikas seemed fantastically easy. There were big crowds of Arabs on either side. But they made no attempt to interfere.

The avenue gave on to a shorter and slightly narrower street of looted open-fronted stalls. It had been a market place of a better type than that used by most Arabs. Almost certainly it was the European shopping centre.

Except for a handful of semi-naked children and a couple of diseased beggars, there were no people here.

Near the end of the street, which took a slight bend, Horfal had to order a resumption of normal marching pace. There were two reasons. One was that Laubert seemed in danger of being tossed out of his litter. The other that, between the stalls, he had glimpsed relatively tall, modern buildings. Which indicated that they were near the governmental centre of Baikas. Near the legation. Caution was again needed.

But he did not anticipate the abruptness with which they found themselves on the edge of a large square.

Horfal gave the order and they halted.

None in the detachment had served in Baikas during the French occupation. Thus the extent of western influence in this part of the city came as a surprise. It was the more impressive because of impact and contrast. They saw a clear, almost noble, space of two hundred yards across. It was well paved. In the centre a natural fountain still played into a damaged marble pool. Around the shallow water lay four prostrate monuments to notable French soldiers and statesmen. On three sides of the square stood dominating and tapering pilasters which served the purely ethereal purpose of hiding the squalor of the alleys beyond.

And on the fourth side — directly opposite them — were the official buildings. These were a row of some half-dozen red sandstone structures, two or three floors high.

The one on the extreme left was slightly smaller than the others and stood apart. It was protected by tall iron rails. From the top of it the Tricolour slumped lazily in the still evening air.

This was the legation.

The mob was still around it. They clustered deep in front of it and down each side as far as the eye could see. Beyond them, almost pressed against the rails, an occasional smudge of grey could be discerned. That, Horfal decided, must be the Hanah militia. He felt almost affectionate towards them. Certainly he felt deeply grateful. For it seemed that they had succeeded in keeping the mob out of the building.

'We're not too late,' Horfal said to no one and everyone.

'The legation's safe.'

He did not notice Lydia. None of them did. She stared at the buildings in a puzzled way. Then, reluctantly, she left Laubert. She took an uncertain pace towards Horfal and stood at his side. He was suddenly aware of her presence. But he did not look directly at her. He did not want to be bothered by her. He was watching the mob. As he had expected, they were turning away from the legation and facing towards the detachment. They were coalescing into a solid mass. In a few moments they would advance across the hundred yards which separated them from the legionnaires.

Lydia said: 'Sergeant Horfal, I . . . '

'Talk to me later!'

'There is . . . '

'*Senorita!* Can't you see we have more trouble on our hands? We have to get through that rabble before we can get into the embassy! Leave me alone!'

Her blue eyes narrowed, became a shade darker. Then she swore at him. The oaths were partly Arabic, partly French. They were searingly lurid and comprehensive.

She broke off abruptly. Then she said: 'I was going to tell you that when I was here before the people surrounded all the buildings. Now they are only round the French building. Do you understand — you big pig?'

Horfal understood.

This meant that the wretched government of Hanah itself must have been compelled to seek refuge in the legation. And the few Arab troops round it were the last remnant of their authority. In other words, thirty-four weary legionnaires plus a sprinkling of Arab soldiers were the last strongpoint of sanity in the whole of the country. All the rest was murder, looting, chaos.

Horfal had an idea that there were other implications, too. But he had no time to consider them. This new mob — greatly larger than the last — was less than fifty yards away. They were approaching like a solid wall. And, in contrast to the experience of a few minutes before, they were almost completely silent. They bore the stamp of men who were well versed in butchery. This was surely the hard core of the revolution.

Most of them were armed. Well armed, in many cases. They held rifles and pistols which must have been seized from government dumps, or from their own soldiers.

Horfal looked over their heads. He could see the legation more clearly now. He could see the tall gates. The small quadrangle beyond. The shuttered windows.

In there were the people they had been sent to protect . . . His orders were to avoid conflict with the Arabs.

He'd done his best to observe that order, he told himself. Since entering this filthy country they had not fired a shot. They had acted like saints! But even saints had their limits . . .

He was going to enter that legation. And he was going to do so quickly . . .

No more of this edging through the rabble!

'*Fusil!*'

The order was obeyed with alacrity. It was the sort of order they had been hoping to hear. The Lebels swung up. First sightings were taken into the depth of the mob. Horfal noticed this instinctive aiming and smiled.

'Not yet!' he shouted. 'They'll have a chance. Put two rounds over their heads . . . *fire!*'

Because of the surrounding buildings, the explosions produced were shattering. As the first volley began to echo, the second joined with it. Every legionnaire felt his eardrums vibrate. A thin cloud of cordite smoke formed round them.

Then silence again. A dazed, stupefied silence, in which the rabble halted as though controlled by puppet strings.

Horfal did not wait.

'Forward . . . at the double!'

The Arabs spread out, forming a

concave like the spreading of a fan. The detachment drove into the depth of it. But a considerable body of them were still in front of the legation gates.

'*Halt!*'

The legionnaires came to a slithering, uneven stop. Horfal gestured towards the rabble directly in front.

'Another round . . . over their heads, but let them feel the breeze!'

It is always difficult to aim a rifle accurately when it is supporting a bayonet. Particularly a Lebel.

Thus it might have been accidental that a few of the shots were too low. That the slugs drilled through turbaned heads. But Horfal was not concerned with such niceties of discipline. He was only impressed by the result. For suddenly the way was open. The gates were a mere twenty yards ahead and nothing to stop them getting there. Only seven or eight very still bodies reminded them of that faction of the mob.

Nothing to stop them?

Except, perhaps, the Hanah militiamen.

They were pressed against the railings. They were fingering their rifles. They were looking wildly and confusedly at the legionnaires. The last thing that Horfal wanted was to get into conflict with them. They were his only potential allies. It was they who, with considerable courage, had shielded the legation.

He shouted something to them in Arabic. Even as he blurted the words, he was not sure what they were, save that they were meant to be reassuring. And they seemed to have that effect. For as they reached the gates the Arab soldiers lowered their rifles. One of them, who appeared to be in command, came running up. His normally dark brown face was tinged with grey through fatigue and anxiety

Horfal decided that this was an instance when he must be militarily correct. He came to attention and saluted. The Arab officer was momentarily nonplussed. Then he touched his turban. The formality completed, Horfal continued to keep the initiative.

'We are here to protect the French nationals in this legation,' *he* said decisively. 'Whatever you have been told, that is our only purpose.'

'But this is sovereign territory. It is no

longer a French protectorate. You have no right within our borders.'

Horfal's knowledge of international law was hazy. But he made a guess. It was a good one.

'We have every right to be here to protect our own people when your government can't do so. Now please do not waste time . . . these gates are locked. Can you open them?'

The Arab officer shook his head. Horfal muttered something profane. He realised that the only people to hold the key to the stout steel lock would be the legation staff. And in all probability they were unaware that the legionnaires had arrived, since the windows were shuttered.

Horfal glanced over his shoulder. Time was running out. The mob was recovering from the first shock. Now they were easing towards the rails, cautiously but inexorably. The legionnaires were drawn up in a single column facing them. The four litter bearers with Laubert and Lydia were huddled behind the column.

It dawned on Horfal that the Arab soldiers had been assisted in their efforts to protect the building because at least some of the mob would have a certain reluctance to attack their own countrymen. But now that they were joined by the legionnaires, such sentimental considerations would no longer apply.

Horfal raised his rifle and aimed it at the steel lock. The first bullet twisted it, but did not break it. He re-cocked the Lebel, tried again. This attempt was successful. The entire mechanism disintegrated. Under the impact, the gates swung open of their own volition.

He gave a hand signal to the legionnaires. The file jogged into the courtyard.

Horfal turned again to the Arab officer. He said: 'You can't stay out there now.'

The Arab gave a sickly smile. He was a brave man, but he was unnerved by the speed of events. Hitherto he had merely been doing his duty in trying to protect a neutral building which contained the skulking members of his government as well as Frenchmen. But now his position was hopelessly compromised. He and his men had made no attempt to resist the legionnaires. Therefore it would appear to the mob that they were in collusion with the Legion. This was the sort of polemical material upon which fanatics thrived. The Arab knew it. And he knew that they would not survive many more minutes if they remained at their present stations.

He shouted an Arabic order. It was passed along the line of his militia, who were spaced about a yard apart. The Arab soldiers streamed into the courtyard from each side, forming a secondary file beside the legionnaires. The manoeuvre was completed without casualties, although the air was now raucous with yells of massed fury.

Horfal ran an experienced eye along the line of Arab soldiers. There was nearly a hundred of them. That was excellent. And obviously they were the cream of Hanah republic's armed forces, for their discipline was first-class.

The Arab officer slammed shut the gates, though there was little point in doing so.

He followed with another order. The Arab militia spread out. They formed a new ring round the small building. But now that they were inside the tall rails there was no possibility of being rushed. Any attack through the limited space presented by the damaged gates could be contained easily enough.

Horfal jerked a thumb at the legation. Then he bawled in the Arab's ear so as to be heard above the gathering tumult:

'Is this the only building that's not in the hands of the mob?'

'We still hold our main barracks.'

'You do? Where are they?'

'Behind this legation.'

'How many men have you there?'

'One hundred.'

'Are you in command?'

'I am in temporary command — under the orders of our President, Bav Usta.'

Horfal recalled hearing about the disreputable President of the Hanah republic. But for the moment that person seemed of no importance. Horfal was reassuring himself with the thought that if all went well he would have a force of about two hundred well-trained Arab soldiers as allies. Between them, he told himself, it might be possible to restore some sort of order. But the officer's next shouted statement destroyed Horfal's optimism.

He said: 'I want you to know that my men will not help the soldiers of France in any way — unless Bav Usta orders us to do so. And I do not think he will do that.'

Horfal took off his *kepi*, wiped his wet forehead. The Arab had spoken firmly but without enthusiasm. In the manner of a soldier who remains loyal to his commander, whatever may be his personal opinion of him.

'That will be settled later,' Horfal said. 'Now listen to me . . . I am Sergeant Horfal, and I have taken charge because, as you can see, our captain is seriously injured. And my men are very tired. They need food and rest. Will you continue to protect this building while I take my detachment inside?'

The Arab nodded slowly.

'My name is Otan. By your system of ranking, I am a colonel. As one soldier to another I say that we will protect this building unless our President orders otherwise.'

'Are all our people inside the legation?'

Otan nodded.

Horfal left him, strode towards the file of legionnaires. For the first time he realised how utterly weary they looked, standing there. Now that they were temporarily safe, they had instinctively relaxed. They looked old from exhaustion and nerve strain — all of them. Even the youngest. The litter bearers, who had suffered an acute sense of helplessness, were the most worn of all.

The girl . . .

It was difficult at this moment to see how she was reacting. For she was again bending over Laubert. Her face was half-hidden by the fall of her fair hair.

'*Repos!*'

The legionnaires ordered arms in response to Horfal's order.

Horfal appreciated that — much as he wished to do so — he could not march all of them into the legation immediately. He would have to make arrangements for them first. But there must be no further delay in moving Laubert inside. The woman, too. And he decided to take the English legionnaire with him for the first contact with the legation staff. Horfal was shrewd enough to appreciate that diplomats would speak a type of French with which he was not familiar. Legionnaire Sayle's knowledge of the tongue would be invaluable.

He gave a further order. Sayle fell out of file, stood beside the litter bearers. Then, led by Horfal, the little group trudged towards the legation doors.

As they reached them, they heard bolts being drawn inside. When they opened, an elderly Arab manservant stood there. He was shaking inside his *burnous* so that the material gave a rustling accompaniment to the chattering of his teeth. They pushed past him.

They were in a surprisingly-large vestibule. And the place was eerie. Their clumsy boots sank into the unfamiliar feel of a thick maroon carpet, making no noise. The walls were painted cool white and draped with tapestries and immense oil portraits. And, because the windows were shuttered, it was gloomy in there. Emergency oil lamps, looking crude amid the opulence, gave a wavering and inadequate light.

They stopped, blinked uncertainly

about them, as the servant re-locked the doors.

Then a door at the far end of the vestibule opened.

A massive shape emerged.

A shape contained in a *burnous* of purple silk. It seemed to glide rather than walk towards them. As it got close they saw that this repulsively-corpulent Arab was smiling. But it was not a pleasing smile. It was more in the nature of a lewd grimace spread across a smooth round face which was ridiculously small in comparison to the body.

The Arab spoke in French — very good French. He said: 'Am I again looking upon soldiers of *La Legio Étrangère?*'

Horfal ignored the question.

'I want to report to the French *chargé*. Take me to him.'

The Arab folded his arms across his great chest. His grimace became rather more emphatic.

'I am not a menial, sergeant. You are not to be expected to know, but permit me to tell you that you are addressing Bav Usta, President of the republic of Hanah.'

Horfal was slightly discomfited. This first meeting had not improved his opinion of the President who had allowed his country to sink into a shambles. But he had made an unfortunate start.

'I am sorry. But I must speak at once to our *chargé*.'

'Why?'

'Why? Because we have come here to protect the French nationals who have taken refuge in this legation.'

The parody of a smile was suddenly gone. Bav Usta's face became blank, utterly expressionless.

He said: 'The French *charge d'affairé*, with his staff and all the other French nationals, are in the basement of this building.'

Horfal could not conceal his surprise. It seemed, to state the case mildly, unbecoming that the representatives of France should hide below ground.

Bav Usta added: 'You are confused — that is natural. But the regrettable fact is that I have found it necessary to take control of this legation. The French nationals are held *incommunicado*.'

This was too much for Horfal fully to comprehend. He glanced desperately at Brian, who was standing close beside him. Brian took the cue.

He said to Bav Usta: 'Do you mean they are held prisoner?'

'In a sense — yes. They are my prisoners. I intend to use them to restore my authority in Hanah. Just as I intend to use you legionnaires. It is an extreme measure, but the alternative for me is death at the hands of the rabble. I will use any device to avoid that.'

10

The Hard Diplomacy

At first they did not see the Hanah
soldiers who gathered round them. They
emerged from the several doors round the
vestibule. Fully a score of them. Silently,
they took stations along the walls. They
held rifles from the waist. They were
aimed at Horfal's tiny group.

It was Lydia who drew attention to them.
She gave a gasp, then pointed to them with
a shaking finger.

Horfal said softly to the legionnaires:
'Keep still — we can't do anything.'

That was true enough. The litter bearers
(for convenience in carrying their burden)
had their Lebels slung across their backs.
Before entering the legation, Horfal and
Brian had done the same. It had seemed a
natural courtesy when entering a diplo-
matic building. But the result was that
they were completely helpless. They could

be shot down before they touched the Lebel slings. And the main body of the detachment was waiting outside, unaware of what was happening.

After giving the cautionary order, Horfal glared about him helplessly. He knew that he was in no way equipped to grapple with this situation. He muttered to Brian: 'This . . . this is a nightmare! Talk . . . find out what it is about . . . '

But Bav Usta had overheard. He said in his fluent French: 'It is no nightmare, sergeant. The facts are simple. In their stupidity the rabble out there wish to kill me. They have gradually seized control of the entire country, and now only this building and the barracks, with a handful of my soldiers, remain. My soldiers, of course, are loyal because they know they will share my fate if the rabble lays hands on them. So . . . '

Brian interrupted. 'We know that. And we're not very interested. But there are two questions that need clearing up. What made you move into this building, which under international law is French territory? And why have you interfered with the representatives of the French government? That's an outrage!'

'I will answer both questions. I moved into this legation because it is easier for my soldiers to defend a small area than a large one. The transfer was completed this morning.'

'With the *chargé's* permission?'

'With his permission. It was done very correctly — at first. Now I will be frank. I knew that the one chance of my survival lay in diverting the hatred of the people from myself. When I heard that the French government was sending legionnaires here to protect the legation I saw my opportunity. I intended to present this as a new French occupation — which the people would bitterly resent. So I deployed a body of troops to observe your approach, then spread the story. I anticipated that the country would become re-united under my leadership in the face of external aggression. But — I miscalculated, although I am still not sure where.'

'I can tell you,' Brian said with some satisfaction. 'Most of your troops were killed or captured before they could do too much harm.'

Bav Usta spread his plump hands out in the gesture of a man who accepts the fates.

'I thought as much, although I could not be certain of it. But this morning, when it became clear that my original plan had failed, I resolved on a new one which occurred to me after I had moved in here. Since it was obvious that you legionnaires would arrive, and that your numbers would not be great, I decided to seize you and offer you to the rabble.'

An old-fashioned French clock stood in a corner of the vestibule. Brian was suddenly aware of its ticking as he said in a strangled fashion: 'What good would that do you? It's you they want — you and your corrupt government!'

'Not entirely. The anti-French feeling runs very deep in Hanah, and it has been fanned by the leaders of the rabble. It will count very much in my favour when I hand over to them a section of French troops who have dared to enter our territory. They will, of course, amuse themselves with you. Probably they will kill you very slowly — but that is not my concern.'

'Suppose . . . suppose you did that. It would give them something new to think about for a few hours, perhaps. But they would still want you.'

'You are too hasty. You have not heard all that I have to say. When I have presented you to the mob, I will take advantage of the new situation to invite the revolutionary leaders in here to meet me. I will dangle a good bait, and I have no doubt that curiosity will induce them to accept. My soldiers will slay them. Thus in two clear strokes I will have given the rabble proof of my patriotism and deprived them of their leadership. Under such circumstances, the revolt must fade out. Gradually, the armed forces of Hanah will reform and I will restore my authority.'

Brian looked at Horfal. The sergeant was studying the maroon carpet at his feet. His expression was beyond description. He looked at the four other legionnaires. They were standing beside the litter. They only partly comprehended what had been said, but their faces were startled masks.

Finally, he looked at Lydia. She was

whispering to Laubert. Her lovely mouth was close to the bandages which crossed over his ear. He realised that she was repeating to him what Bav Usta had said.

Suddenly, from his position prone on the stretcher, Laubert spoke. His voice was toneless with pain. But the words were clear. The first composed words he had spoken since he lost his sight. Because they were so unexpected, they were astounding.

He asked: 'Tell me, Bav Usta, what are your plans for the civilians? I understand they are your prisoners. Do you intend to offer them to the mob, too?'

Bav Usta regarded Laubert for a long moment, his cold eyes studying the rank badges. Then he asked: 'Are you in command of the legionnaires?'

Laubert answered through white lips.

'I am. Now answer my question.'

'Certainly. When I took control of this legation I told the staff and the French nationals that I was doing so for their own protection. I pointed out that they would be safer below ground. They protested, but they had no choice. I needed them out of the way so I could deal directly

216

with you when you arrived . . . '

'*Dieu!* Will you answer me?'

'You are too impatient, *capitaine*. I am doing so. When order is restored in this city, I will have this legation burned down. The civilians, I fear, will still be in the basement. In due course I will report to the French Foreign Office that the place was destroyed by the mob — just as you soldiers were destroyed after reaching here.'

For a moment Laubert raised his bandaged head, as if about to struggle off the litter. But Lydia pushed him back. She did so gently. She whispered something to him. He subsided, his strength gone.

Bav Usta added: 'So you will understand that the mob will be held to blame for all that has happened. No doubt the French Government will demand immediate retribution. I will satisfy them by executing any remaining revolutionary leaders who may have eluded me.'

Horfal extended a long hand. He grasped Bav Usta's robes. The Arab did not move. Horfal spoke through closed teeth.

'When we arrived here I thought your

soldiers were brave men. I spoke to their officer; his name was Otan. I thought he was a man I could respect. Now I know that even they are corrupted in a barbarous country, for no soldiers worthy of that name would help you in such infamy . . . '

Bav Usta pulled away from Horfal. He said: 'My soldiers do not like what they have to do. Otan protested when I told him he must act a part so you would not suspect you were walking into a trap. But he realised he had no alternative.'

'There are nearly thirty legionnaires out there! Do you think they will surrender to your militia so as to be delivered to the mob?'

'They are outnumbered. They are surrounded. And you, sergeant, are not with them to give inspiration and direction. What else can they do? Come with me, sergeant, and I think you'll see that they are already disarmed . . . '

Bav Usta moved to one of the windows. Horfal and Brian followed. The Arab unfastened and drew back the heavy internal shutters. They gazed out into the front courtyard.

It was almost dusk now, with the sun spraying gold on the ravaged city. And the mob beyond the rails were oddly quiet. They were watching . . .

Watching as the soldiers of Hanah formed a ring of rifles round the baffled and helpless legionnaires.

Watching as Otan moved along the file, pulling the Lebels from their grasp.

Watching while several of the legionnaires jerked away and moved as if to resist. They were clubbed down from behind . . .

Bav Usta closed the shutters.

'They will be joining you,' he said. 'And all of you will spend tonight in the basement with the civilians. Tomorrow, with due ceremony, I will deliver you trussed like chickens to the mob.'

★   ★   ★

The basement had been used for storing legation documents. There were several hundreds of these, rolled and tied with tape and put into filing cabinets which fringed the walls. They gave a ridiculously official appearance to a place which was foetid, crowded and tense.

Now that the legionnaires had arrived, there were nearly a hundred people in the place, which was lighted by a single lamp from the low ceiling.

They sprawled on the sandstone floor — a peculiar conglomeration of uniforms and civilian clothes. They slept. They talked in undertones. They argued. And over them all was an atmosphere of fearful unreality. The unreality of impending death. For death is a state which always applies to someone else. Never to oneself.

Horfal . . .

He was standing in the centre of the floor. He was talking in undertones with the French *chargé*. They contrasted greatly, those two. The filthy, unshaven sergeant. The precise, plump little diplomat.

Horfal had never had contact with such an eminent person before. Normally, he might have been tongue-tied in such a presence. But not now. Not under these circumstances. For the third time he was explaining all that had happened in answer to the *chargé's* bewildered queries.

Lydia . . .

She was with Laubert in a corner near the door, so that he could get some cool air from the draught. She was holding his head in her arms as he lay on the litter. And she was listening to him. Listening while Lauber spoke in broken whispers.

Laubert . . .

He did not know why he was talking to her. He did not care. But he found it a relief to tell of his play with the revolver which contained just one bullet. To explain to her that it had been the one way he had been able to get relief from the tension which built up within him while he was held in that fort.

Now he knew a new and strange relief. It came out of his own personal and perpetual darkness. And out of the cool arms which he could not see, but which were holding him. Protecting him. Understanding him.

This from the woman who had blinded him . . .

Sometimes he paused in the disconnected tale he was telling to wonder at the miracle which had given him, in this of all times, a sense of peace he had never known before. A feeling that someone cared for him . . .

Brian . . .

He was standing beside the door, next to a legation clerk, watching Lydia.

The slim, small body, its outlines showing clearly beneath those ragged robes.

It was an infamy that such a creature should have been condemned to the squalor of a primitive Arab town! In proper clothes, against a proper background, she would be a thing of glory and fascination.

And now she was fastening herself utterly to Laubert! It was madness — unjust. She must be doing it out of a sense of shame. But she need not feel ashamed. Laubert was bad. All bad.

Why listen to him while he whispered insults and lies in her ears . . . ?

The legation clerk was speaking to him. Brian listened reluctantly.

'My watch has stopped . . . what's the time?'

Brian glanced at his own watch.

'Nine o'clock,' he said. And he thought: 'About twelve hours before they hand us over to the mobs.'

* * *

The brigadier-general was working late. It was with a sigh of relief that he signed the last memorandum and handed it to his aide.

'What time is it?' he asked.

'Nine o'clock, *mon generale.*'

'Any word from Baikas yet?'

'*Non.*'

'Laubert's column ought to be there by now . . . has there been any signal from the legation today?'

'Nothing since last night.'

'Then the position can't be any worse, or they'd have let us know. But we'd better keep in touch . . . have an enquiry signal sent through immediately and let me know the result. I'll be taking dinner in the mess . . . '

* * *

An Arab signals expert had taken over the legation radio room. He reported to Bav Usta.

'This has come in from Sidi Bel Abbes,'

he said, handing over a slip of paper.

Bav Usta read it carefully.

Then, after a few moments' thought, he dictated a reply.

'Transmit it immediately,' Bav Usta said.

★ ★ ★

At fifteen minutes past ten the brigadier-general was sipping his post-dinner brandy. His aide disturbed him.

'I have the reply from Baikas, *mon generale.*'

'Let me see it.'

The brigadier-general studied the slip. It read '*Legion column has just arrived. Mob has been threatening to burn legation, but presence of French troops has quietened them. President Bav Usta is co-operating fully and courageously with Captain Laubert in efforts to restore order.*'

The brigadier-general looked reflectively at the ceiling.

'I don't like those threats to burn the legation,' he said. 'It seems the column has arrived only just in time. But I feel we will receive more reassuring news tomorrow.'

Lieutenant Du Pois sat on the edge of his bunk. He was talking urgently to the medical officer.

'I'm worried,' he repeated. 'Very worried. The last thing Laubert said was that he would send a signal when he reached the legation. There's been no signal, and he ought to be there by now.'

The M.O. drew at his rank pipe, then ejected a stream of stupefying smoke at a sand fly.

'They'll be all right,' he said confidently.

'How can you say that when Laubert's last words . . .'

'I know, I know. But it is only just ten o'clock. He can't have been there many hours. And he's probably had a lot to do. There'll be plenty on Laubert's mind without rushing to the radio transmitter to satisfy your youthful curiosity, *mon ami*. But since you are so concerned, why don't you send a signal yourself? The wavelength will be in the radio room lists.'

Du Bois boggled at the thought.

'I send a signal to a French legation? It

is impossible! They would think it insolence! I dare not do it. But I know what I will do . . . I will send an enquiry to the High Command. I don't think they'll object.'

Half an hour later . . .

'It's all right,' Du Bois said happily. 'I've just had a reply from the High Command. They say the column has arrived safely. *Tiens!* I'm glad. But . . . but I wish Laubert had let me know himself . . . '

★　★　★

Bav Usta had occupied the *chargé's* private living room. There he sat in an armchair, his robes flowing over the sides, while he considered and analysed his plans. It was unfortunate that the woman kept obtruding in his thoughts. She was a desirable little animal who had come in with the column . . .

Probably communal property among the legionnaires, he told himself. But very attractive. He had had very little opportunity to think about her until now. And now he was curious. She was white? Then why was she wearing a *burnous?* Where did she come from? With an effort he forced her from his mind. Deliberately, he reconsidered his manoeuvres for the morrow.

There was a small balcony off this room. It looked out on the city square. Tomorrow morning, as soon as the crowds were thick again, he was going to speak to the mob from that balcony. Bav Usta was a considerable orator. He had no doubt that his powerful voice and his practised periods would command their attention once the immediate screaming had died down.

He would tell them that their miseries were due to the ruthless swindling of the French businessmen and engineers who remained in Baikas. The French, he would explain, had continued to bleed their country dry even after the military occupation had ended. That sort of simple argument would appeal to a rabble. Then he would tell them that his heart was with them. He regretted that the people of Hanah, through no fault of his own, had been divided against each other. He felt no bitterness to any of them . . .

After that would come the critical

moment. He would remind them that the French had thought fit to enter their sovereign territory. That he, Bav Usta, by a subtle manoeuvre, had disarmed and captured them.

Even in this moment he had protected his people against the fury of French arms! Was that not proof of his devotion to the common people of the land?

Bav Usta rubbed a tear from his gross cheek as he considered the moving appeal he would make.

Then he would announce that he was handing over the legionnaires to the justice of the people.

With that, he would withdraw.

And the legionnaires, their hands lashed behind their backs, would be brought out and pushed through the gates.

He would allow time for the excitement to die down. Then he would make a second appearance on the balcony. This time he would make an earnest appeal to end bloodshed. He would invite the leaders of the rabble in to talk with him.

They would accept, after such proof of his patriotism. And quietly, without the rabble knowing, they would be put to death. If any of them asked where their leaders were, he would tell them any suitable story. Bav Usta knew that an illiterate mass would believe almost anything. And ultimately, without anyone to guide them, and with a new feeling of respect for their President, they would disperse. The next step would be to move out of the legation and back to the government buildings.

When that was done, the legation would be set ablaze. Little would remain of the French civilians in the basement. Bav Usta calculated that within two or three days, as his army re-formed, he would regain absolute control.

And then he would transmit an urgent message to the French Government. It would explain that the Legion column was dragged out of the embassy by the furious population and lynched. And later, despite the efforts of his troops, the civilians perished in the burning legation, fired by the mob.

As he had explained to Captain Laubert, the French demand for retaliatory action against the mob would be a convenient excuse for getting rid of the remaining agitators.

Regarded as a whole, the plan was without flaw. It could only result in he, Bav Usta, having more complete authority than ever before. For he would appear to the population as the man who had rid their country of the French. True, rumours might, in time, reach the ears of the French authorities. But they could do nothing on the basis of hearsay. And there would be no witnesses — no French witnesses — of what had in fact occurred.

There was no possibility of any last-minute hitch. His radio signal must have satisfied the French High Command. It had been carefully phrased so as to prepare the atmosphere for incendiarism while at the same time showing himself in a light of blameless dedication to duty.

But even if the French were not satisfied. Even if they suspected that all was not well in Baikas, they could do nothing. Bav Usta knew that no troops were immediately available for a second entry into the country. And they were far out of range of the small French air fleet based in Morocco.

Where did that woman come from . . . ?

Bav Usta now felt entitled to give his whole attention to that minor but intriguing question.

He decided that it would be shameful, even wasteful, to allow her to die with the legionnaires. But — if she lived she would be a white witness. She would know not only what had happened, but precisely why it had happened. And if at any time the French authorities got in touch with her, the repercussions for the President of the Hanah republic might be embarrassing.

Anyway, these were questions which could only be decided after speaking to the girl herself. He would send for her . . .

* * *

Bav Usta regarded her from the depth of his chair. He surveyed her slim, tense form as a dealer might inspect an animal in a cattle market.

He said: 'I have sent for you because I am curious. There is no need to be afraid of me — are you afraid?'

She was standing a little distance from him, with her back to the shuttered window. There were shadows in her eyes.

'There is no need to be curious about me — I am not important.'

Bav Usta drummed his fingers on his enormous knee.

'You speak French very badly. Where do you come from?'

In a brief sentence she told him. He smiled his satisfaction. Clearly, the girl would be no menace if she lived. She was not a French subject. She was a mere waif. No one would listen to her.

When he next spoke he did so in Arabic.

'You know what is going to happen to the legionnaires?'

She nodded, her eyes never leaving him.

'But you would not want to die with them?'

She did not answer. But she continued to stare at him. Bav Usta found it disconcerting. She had the appearance of one who was sleeping with eyes open.

'Answer me! Do you want to die?'

'Does anyone want to die? That is the question of a fool that you ask!'

Bav Usta controlled his annoyance. He told himself that it was good to have a woman of spirit. He said: 'You need not do so — if you are reasonable with me.'

Her voice purred as she asked: 'What does that mean?'

'What does any man mean when he talks to such a woman as you?'

Suddenly she turned away so that her back was to him. She whispered: 'I do not want those legionnaires to die . . .'

Bav Usta toyed with the jewelled hilt of his knife. He said smoothly: 'I cannot make conditions. They are going to die. The question is whether you are going to do so with them.'

'There is one man . . . the officer . . . he is blind . . . surely he . . .'

'There can be no exceptions, so please don't try to discuss them.'

With an ungainly effort, Bav Usta rose from the chair. He advanced on Lydia, towering over her. She still had her back to him. He closed his massive, clumsy arms round her small waist. She did not move. He drew her close to the repulsive softness of his body.

There was no resistance. But she said: 'I wish to speak to the captain. Just for the last time . . . will you do that for me?'

'Why so much concern for one who is blind?'

'Will you let me see him — first. In here if you wish. After that . . . I do not care what happens.'

He shrugged his shoulders. Then he left her reluctantly and rang the handbell on a table.

★ ★ ★

Laubert was guided in by one of the Arab soldiers. Bav Usta dismissed the soldier. Then he watched with mild amusement as Laubert stumbled forward, hands held in front.

Lydia went to him. Gently, she escorted him to the chair in which Bav Usta had been sitting. Then she turned to the Arab.

'Look at him,' she said. 'Come closer

234

. . . would you kill such a man as he?'

Bav Usta smiled. 'You thought to appeal to my sympathy again.'

'If you have any — yes. I say that no man can look upon Captain Laubert and condemn him to the death you plan. Come close and look, I say . . . or are you too squeamish to watch such a face?'

There was a soft compulsion in her voice. Bav Usta approached the chair.

'Do you see the bandage over his eyes?'

'Of course I do.'

'Touch it . . . touch the bandage and I will tell you something which will surprise you. Do it . . . unless you are afraid of a Frenchman who cannot see . . . '

He gave a deprecating laugh. Then he extended a hand.

At the moment it made contact with his face, Laubert sprang forward. His groping fingers found Bav Usta's throat. His thumbs pressed on it. It was a mad grip which could not be broken.

Before he died, a far-off voice reached Bav Usta's agonised brain. It was her voice. It was saying: 'Now I will tell you . . . it was I who blinded him . . . '

And then Lydia went to the door. There was an Arab soldier outside. She said to him: 'President Bav Usta wants to speak with Colonel Otan.'

She closed the door before the request could be queried.

And when Otan came, they showed him the body of Bav Usta. Then Laubert spoke to him as one soldier to another.

11

The Sacrifice

The door of the basement prison swung open. Colonel Otan stood on the threshold. He surveyed them with a strained face. Then he held up his hands to quieten the hub-bub of voices.

'Listen to me carefully,' he said in French. 'There is little time, and you must understand well. First — Bav Usta is dead. He was killed by your Captain Laubert.'

In a few phrases he outlined what had happened in the *chargé's* room. They listened in stunned silence. The silence of those who want to believe, but are not sure that they do.

Then he continued: 'I am not going to pass judgment on such a slaying. I am only concerned that the President is no longer alive. Therefore there is no possibility of retrieving power from the rabble. The revolution must run its course. That can only mean death for we who have served the President — if we stay here.'

Brian voiced the thought which had sprung into all of their minds.

'Do you mean that we — all of us — might get out?'

'I think it is possible. Captain Laubert has outlined a plan.'

'Where is Laubert?'

'He is making preparations. The woman is with him. They are safe and unharmed.'

Brian said quickly: 'How can we be sure of that? Why aren't they here?'

'It is their wish to be alone. And it is Captain Laubert's orders that you do exactly as I say. You must believe me . . . now are you ready to listen?'

Horfal said: 'We'll listen — but it does not mean that we will believe.'

'I think I will convince you when I return your rifles to your legionnaires.'

'*Santa!* You will do that?'

'I will. Now heed what I say . . . ' Otan gathered himself. Then he continued: 'I have under my command two hundred soldiers. There are more than thirty of you legionnaires. Together we would make a strong force to break out of Baikas, even though we would have to protect your civilians.'

Brian looked unimpressed. He said: 'It seems too simple to me. We only reached this place because we had the advantage of surprise. The mob would have plenty of warning before we broke out of this building. Even two hundred armed men might not get through.'

'It is night — the rabble are not so thick around the building.'

'They will still be thick enough. It might be worth trying, but I don't think much of our chances. Not unless something can be done to divert the mob's attention — and there's no way of doing that.'

'Captain Laubert says that there is.'

'You mean . . . Laubert is planning a diversion? What is it?'

Otan shook his head.

'Before Allah, I say I do not know. He would not say. But he told me to tell you that he relies on you to join with me in leaving this building at fifteen minutes after midnight. That is the hour he gave me. He said there must be no mistake. No delay. He said that whatever happens, we must leave then.'

Horfal thrust forward. He asked urgently: 'But where will Laubert be? And the girl?'

'He says they have their own plans for escape.'

Horfal and Brian looked at each other. Doubt was reflected in their faces. Then they were aware of a movement among the civilians. All of them were standing. Hope radiated from them.

Horfal said: 'It is not ourselves we must think about. We must not even think about Laubert and the girl. Our duty is to the people who took refuge in this legation. We were sent here to protect them, and we have failed. We must take any opportunity of saving them now.'

Brian nodded. Then he said to Otan: 'The girl . . . are you sure she's all right? Can I not see her?'

'She is all right, legionnaire. But you cannot see her. She is alone with Laubert . . . do you understand . . . ?'

Brian thought that he did. And because suddenly he no longer hated Laubert, he no longer felt the sears of jealousy.

Arab soldiers came into the basement. They staggered under the weight of the legionnaires' rifles and equipment. They were deposited in a confused heap in the centre of the floor.

But that confused heap meant everything.

It meant that this was no trap. It meant that there was again hope. That Otan had spoken truthfully.

They worked at feverish speed to sort out the mass of webbing straps, water-bottles, valises, ammunition pouches and Lebels.

Otan watched. And Brian said to him: 'Suppose we get out of Baikas. What about you people? Your soldiers, I mean. What will you do — where will you go?'

Otan smiled.

'We will escort you to the border of our country . . . '

'And then?'

'And then we will wait where none will see us until the fury has died down. After that — perhaps we will return to Baikas. Perhaps we will help the people to find a new leader who is honourable and whom soldiers can serve with honour. But that is in the future, legionnaire . . . let us only worry about the present.'

They assembled in the vestibule of the legation — the remnants of Hanah's elite Arab troops and thirty-four legionnaires. Plus nearly three score French civilians, some of them women. Outside they were to be joined by the remaining Arab soldiers, who were still forming a protective circle round the building.

By agreement, Horfal was to take general command. Since speed was the main consideration, he had decided on a circular formation, with the civilians in the centre. He foresaw many difficulties in keeping such a formation if the mob pressure became too great. He could only hope that the Arab soldiers would clearly understand what was required of them . . .

But even as he checked and instructed and queried, he kept looking for Laubert. Hoping to see that blind figure . . .

And Brian kept looking for Lydia . . .

★   ★   ★

At exactly fifteen minutes after midnight they emerged out of the main doors and into the courtyard. Rapidly, they made up their formation. It was complete in a single minute. Then they moved through the gates to where they knew the mob waited.

But there was scarcely a mob at all. Only a few knots of Arabs were in front of the gates. So far as they could detect in the darkness, most of the rabble had suddenly concentrated on a point to the right of the legation, leaving the path clear through the main square.

★   ★   ★

At a few minutes before quarter past twelve, Laubert and Lydia left the legation by a side door. He had an arm round her shoulders as they crossed the court yard.

An Arab soldier — obeying instructions from Otan to do whatever Laubert directed — opened a small gate in the rails for them. Laubert got through it with difficulty. Lydia followed.

They were holding each other again as they walked slowly towards the mob.

For a short while the rabble did not react. They gazed in semi-disbelief. Then, from all sides, they closed in on the couple.

Laubert waited. Waited until he could feel them pulling at him. And trying to pull Lydia away from him.

Then he pulled a revolver from his tunic pocket. An old type of English revolver. With just a single cartridge in the chamber.

He groped with the barrel until it was pressed against the back of Lydia's neck. With his thumb he checked that the bullet was in a position to fire.

Then he squeezed the trigger.

THE END

Other titles in the
Linford Mystery Library:

ZONE ZERO

John Robb

Western powers plan to explode a hydro-gen bomb in a remote area of Southern Algeria — code named Zone Zero. The zone has to be evacuated. Fort Ney is the smallest Foreign Legion outpost in the zone, commanded by a young lieutenant. Here, too, is the English legionnaire, tortured by previous cow-ardice, as well as a little Greek who has within him the spark of greatness. It has always been a peaceful place — until the twelve travellers arrive. Now the outwitted garrison faces the uttermost limit of horror . . .

THE WEIRD SHADOW OVER MORECAMBE

Edmund Glasby

Professor Mandrake Smith would be unrecognisable to his former colleagues now: the shambling, drink-addled erstwhile Professor of Anthropology at Oxford is now barely surviving in Morecambe. He has many things to forget, although some don't want to forget him. Plagued by nightmares from his past, both in Oxford and Papua New Guinea, he finds himself drafted by the enigmatic Mr. Thorn, whom he grudgingly assists in trying to stop the downward spiral into darkness and insanity that awaits Morecambe — and the entire world . . .

DEATH BY GASLIGHT

Michael Kurland

London has been shocked by a series of violent murders. The victims are all aristocrats, found inside locked rooms, killed in an identical manner. Suspecting an international plot, the government calls in the services of Sherlock Holmes. Public uproar causes the police to set visible patrols on every street; fear of the murderer looks like putting the criminal class of London out of business! They in turn call in the services of Holmes's nemesis, Professor James Moriarty. What will happen when the two titans clash with the killer?

THE SECOND HOUSE

V. J. Banis

When Liza Durant is saved from drowning by Jeffrey Forrest, she little realizes how much it will change her life. Jeffrey is the heir to the old manor La Deuxieme, the 'second house'. Within days he proposes to Liza, who agrees to visit him at his country home. A series of accidents soon follows, and Liza finds herself in a web of intrigue over the inheritance of the great house. Can she escape alive? Or will the curse of the second house claim yet another victim?

THE MODEL MURDERS

Norman Firth

When Mornia Garish's body was found dead, she became the fifth such victim in two years. The police believed the crimes were the work of a maniac. Then another sinister pattern emerged: they had all recently posed nude for portraits by the artist Gilbert Reeves. Determined to escape from her poor background, Rebecca Kay takes all manner of risks to become a top-line model. But when she agrees to pose for Reeves, has she taken a risk too far?